MANY DROPS MAKE A STREAM

ADRIAN HARLEY

I0642759

DUCK PRINTS PRESS

Schenectady, New York

Many Drops Make a Stream
Copyright © 2023, Adrian Harley

Front cover art © 2023, Roiu Cris

Edited by Nina Waters
Print Manuscript formatting by Hermit Prints
E-book formatting by Nina Waters

Published by Duck Prints Press, LLC
Schenectady, New York
duckprintspress.com

ISBN: 978-1-946472-95-3 (Paperback edition)
ISBN: 978-1-946472-97-7 (ePub edition)
ISBN: 978-1-946472-96-0 (PDF edition)

Tags

Genre: fantasy

Rating: general audiences

Trigger Warnings: character injury (non-graphic descriptions), misgendering (unintentional), speciesism

Relationships: childhood friends, enemies to lovers, f/f, f/f (background), f/f (past), family, found family, pre-relationship

Character Features: amnesia (magical) (temporary), bipoc, bird person, creature-human hybrid, creature transformation (animal), creature transformation (bird), creature transformation (dog), creature transformation (fish), creature transformation (involuntary), criminal, ghost, magic use, magic use (blood magic), necromancy, non-human character, vigilante

Other Tags: be gay do crimes, be gay solve crimes, break-up (past), cults, enslavement, heist, human trafficking, imprisonment, kidnapping, past tense, pov third person limited, religion, rob from the rich to help the poor, summer solstice, there is only one bed

To Mom and Dad

Table of Contents

Chapter One

If Droplet had believed Moss about how much time vigilantes spent waiting around for things to happen, she would have been much less eager to take up the mantle.

Droplet had been patrolling the docks of the city of Ninuthen for hours in the form of a seagrass owl—a local bird, and therefore inconspicuous. She carried a necklace of bones in her talons, but nothing else. Shapeshifters could travel light.

Ninuthen-proper glowed. Every street boasted lamps of light magic, and the wealthier businesses had sprung for glimmering murals that shone from their walls at all hours of the day and night. Nobody wanted to shower such extravagance on the dock quarter, though. Perched in the shadows, Droplet marinated in an agonizing blend of boredom and tension.

When the deep bells of the dockside Sea Goddess temple pealed midnight, Droplet took off from a warehouse roof for another circuit. The smugglers she'd overheard in the tavern had not been obliging enough to say exactly which dock they were using. Nor when they planned to arrive.

Mice, rats, drunken brawl, more mice, a couple having an amorous encounter on a warehouse roof, more rats...there! Finally! Two cloaked, hooded figures pulling a large tarpaulin-covered cart between a couple of warehouses. One human and one raptor—she caught a glimpse of featherless hands from under one robe, and a feathery snout and long tail from beneath another.

Aside from the many tiny bones of her necklace clicking

together, Droplet's midair turn was silent.

The two suspicious characters and their ungainly cart headed for a boatless dock filled with similarly suspicious tarpaulin-covered items. Far out on the bay, hard to spot even with owl eyes, a small ship approached despite furled sails and no oars to be seen. They had a talented water mage on the way, then, at minimum. She would have to be quick. Bone sucked up cast magic like a sponge but could only take so much before it gave up, like a bucket of water against a wildfire.

Droplet flew to the end of the dock. The owl form had served its purpose. Time to shift.

In the first instant of the change, Droplet's body felt stiff, taut, as if her skin was a net that had held her for too long. And then, in the next glorious instant, she broke free. Her muscles and bones and skin *stretched*, the good kind of stretch that popped stiff joints and shook off fatigue. She relaxed into the form of a gorilla—a male goldback weighing in at 400 pounds. Weather-warped, splintering boards creaked under her new knuckles.

When Moss had first let her go on vigilante missions, Droplet had favored big-cat forms. The confidence that came from walking around with literal handfuls of blades was unbeatable. But without opposable thumbs, her most fearsome nemesis had become that wily foe: the closed door. Shifting was nigh-instantaneous, but it took energy, and a shifter always needed a few moments to adjust to the muscles and senses of the new form. Every second mattered in a fight or escape.

Gorillas were no slouches in the "sight and hearing" department, but after the owl, Droplet felt like a blanket had dropped on her head. But the smells of the bay rushed in—the underlying odor of dead fish and dockside trash left something to be desired, and the salty, clean breeze of night blew in off the sea.

No time to waste. The cart-pushers and boat-driver were coming. She put on the bone necklace—she needed her hands free, and the bone wouldn't interfere with any necessary shape-changes. Shapeshifting was a part of her; not even a necromancer could stop her from shifting.

Droplet lifted the tarps. Under them sat three crates sealed against light and sound. Simple spells. Astonishingly, the spellcasters had not thought to spell against a gorilla's arm strength. She grabbed the side of the closest crate and ripped it clean away.

Inside the crate was a person.

A hybrid.

Humans, curse them, probably wouldn't use the word "person" to describe hybrids. Casualties of old magic gone wrong, a blend of at least two different animals and permanently stuck in between, hybrids could be dismissed as "not *really* people" whenever it was convenient for the humans and raptors in charge.

Droplet didn't know why these people were locked up, and she didn't care. She just needed to get them out.

The person in the first crate, by all appearances a normal, large gray dog, growled "Thank you!" before fleeing into the night.

The second crate held a person with a more balanced mixture of cat and human. Her gray tabby fur puffed up all over; tufts extended around the collar of her fish-scale dress and the straps of her sandals, and the Sea Goddess clip on her head stood up vertically. If the situation hadn't been so dire, the effect would have been comical. Her ears lay flat, and her pupils were so wide that her eyes were almost black.

"Okay. Okay. A gorilla. I was not expecting this, but here we are," said the hybrid. Droplet stood back to allow the chattering hybrid out of the narrow box. She slunk out, her fluffed-up tail getting in her face as she emerged. She stood on hind legs nearly as long as a human's but jointed like a cat's, and she stretched as tall as she could, ears flicking in every direction. "They grabbed me at The Mouse's Last Stand and said something about 'quota.' Maybe 'two more until quota'? One said he'd be glad once midsummer was over."

Droplet nodded at the cat's words, encouraging her to continue as she described more of the smells, sights, and sounds she'd observed before she'd been put in the crate. The woman didn't seem to look at the nod but kept narrating anyway, scanning the shore.

The hybrid in the third crate—a feather-covered human—screamed at the sight of a gorilla effortlessly tearing open crates; they leapt past Droplet and dove into the water. Droplet couldn't blame them.

"Look out!" the cat-hybrid shouted, shoving at Droplet's right side like a duckling trying to move a boulder.

Spooked by the touch more than the shout, Droplet jumped to her left and heard something whiz past her ear. She whirled and stood on her hind legs. The cart had arrived at the dock, the two mysterious cart-pullers now armed and ready. The raptor held up their hands, preparing to cast a spell; nothing for Droplet to worry about with her bone charm on.

The human had a crossbow.

Great.

Thankfully, reloading a crossbow took time. And Droplet had been itching to take them head-on.

Droplet dropped to all fours, squared her shoulders, and charged, bellowing as she pounded down the dock, boards shaking under her feet. The raptor mage waved their hands in a quick arc, and a rope of fire whipped through the air toward her. Trusting in her bone necklace, Droplet charged on.

When the fire *did* burn her, sheer momentum kept her barreling down the dock. She bellowed again, instinctively, out of pain.

In a just universe, the sight of a bellowing, charging gorilla who was literally on fire would have sent these people fleeing.

Instead, the mage raised their hands again.

Droplet kept charging for a few more feet, until she smacked into a wall of air with a soft *fwump* that rattled her from head to feet. At least the impact put the fire out. Once stopped in her tracks, she finally realized what was going on.

The mage was using blood magic.

Immensely powerful, immensely illegal, blood magic could do almost anything when the caster had enough willing or unwilling blood donors. Droplet's bone necklace, a formidable shield against the everyday elemental magic she'd thought she'd face, was about as much use as a paper dagger in a pub brawl.

Droplet would have to think her way out of this.

She *hated* thinking her way out.

She weighed her options. None were good. Shifting was only so much help. They'd stopped one of her larger forms with ease; a smaller form would fare no better.

Behind the humans, the cart still held its tarp-covered cargo. At least one person could be under there—maybe more, depending on the species. But the blood mages could be carrying provisions and supplies. A gorilla's senses weren't keen enough to tell the difference, even without the burnt-fur smell interfering. A large broom was painted on the tarp—a street sweeper's cart? Had the blood mages stolen from street sweepers?

In the pause for thought, the pain from the burns settled deeper even though the flames had gone out. And over the lap of water came a distant muttering...

"...and yes, I know this is a bad idea. She can tell me 'I told you so' later," said the cat-hybrid.

With dread in her stomach, Droplet looked over her shoulder.

The hybrid held giant splinters of the crate walls. She tucked them under her arms, took a deep breath, and charged.

"RREEOOOOOW!"

She ran like a person constantly on the edge of tipping over a cliff. She had no real grip on the bulky fragments of wood. And wood absorbed some magic, sure, like any dead matter, but it wasn't as efficient as bone.

The cloaked people exchanged a look. The blood mage left one hand upraised toward Droplet, moving the other toward the cat.

The archer finished reloading the crossbow and raised it to point at Droplet's heart.

With all the strength in her gorilla legs, Droplet leapt right and shifted mid-leap, diving toward the bay. For an instant, she was overstretched, overextended, until her body collapsed in on itself and settled. She became a barracuda. Barracudas were fast—she planned to speed under the docks and come around the other side, taking them by surprise, so she'd have time to shift again, grab the hybrid, and get out of there.

Instead, no more than three feet from the dock, still midair, she thudded into nothing and dropped, disoriented. She splashed into the water. The saltwater. Stars above, she had *not* thought about what that would do to the burn wound. She writhed in the dark water and felt that *thunk* again, different from the air barrier.

The boat! They'd made their getaway boat invisible. She had to get back on the dock now, get the hybrid out before the boat arrived—

A blast of red light and heat seared the water, almost reaching her. Droplet swam under the docks, thanking the stars that this type of fish could navigate in dark water. Picking a fish that could handle these conditions had been pure luck; she tended to avoid her oceanic forms.

No new attack came, but the burn was a constant assault on its own. Droplet steeled herself, dove, and then propelled herself upward, tail beating madly. She broke the surface, arcing toward the dock, and shifted into a tiger midair, as if her rage and anger and pain were taking on weight and claws and fur of their own. Roaring, she landed in a crash and twist of claws digging into wood, barely clearing the dock.

The dock was empty.

The cart was gone.

Even with tiger ears, she heard only the faint slap of water on wood and stone. The smell of burned flesh and fur overwhelmed any subtler scents the boat might have left. The placid water shimmered in the moonlight, unbroken to the horizon.

They couldn't have vanished. That was impossible.

But the illusion was seamless.

Droplet ached from nose to tail, which was decidedly unfair, as she hadn't even had these tailbones until moments ago. She hadn't done such rapid shape-changes in a long time, and her chest and shoulders still screamed, the pain compounded by shifting. Even if she could find the boat, she wouldn't be any good against a blood mage—plus another mage and the archer, at minimum.

Defeated, resigned, she changed into one of her comfort forms: a goose. Although she wouldn't trade the freedom of shapeshifting for anything in this world or beyond, sometimes, after a rough day, a shapeshifter had to rest easy in a body where the limbs and senses were all familiar. Droplet had many goose shapes to choose from, unlike the other species of the evening. She picked the shape of a friend she'd made many years ago whose hobby was terrorizing wealthy mages in their gardens.

Night closed in, goose eyes useless at making out anything other than the garish glow of Ninuthen in the distance, but she could feel the lines of the world, now, stretching beyond the horizon, a better map than anything people could create. And a goose could endure a long flight home.

She took to the air with all the grace and ease of a fish trying to flop its way out of a fisherman's bucket. She flew over the bay once, searching, but to no avail.

Curse them to bloody, nameless chaos, thought Droplet as she begrudgingly turned toward home. *May their mothers learn of their sins and be very disappointed in them.*

Stars, I hope that hybrid's okay.

Chapter Two

Droplet and Moss had settled into a manor west of the city a couple months ago under human personas: an eccentric Nortakian businessperson and her loyal retainer, moved down from the north. Here in Makido, common wisdom held that Nortak was a wild, lawless, icy land ruled by demons. No Makidan questioned why a wealthy Nortakian would move to their vastly superior country.

The nebulous, unspecific cover of "trade" gave Droplet an excuse to talk to the wealthiest humans of the city. One of Moss's first lessons: to find the person responsible for a crime, you looked at the ones with the most money. Conversations and connections with respectable businesspeople had given their former organization most of their leads on where to find and help exploited people.

Like the other manors on this side of town, Droplet's manor dated back several hundred years to the final centuries of the Aulian Empire. It had wide balconies on upper stories—arriving to a gathering by air had been a sign of status for some time. Droplet landed on the eastern balcony and glared at the door leading inside.

We meet again, door handles.

Groaning, she shifted into her human form with the flattest chest for as little distortion to the burn wound as possible. Nonetheless, when she stretched into the new shape, her skin and muscles flared with pain as if the fire had broken out all over again. The burn stood out in angry red against her pale skin. Even lifting her arm toward the door hurt. She gently turned the handle, shuffled inside, and eased the door back shut.

Shapeshifters had an innate gift for language. Droplet knew three different human tongues, and she'd lost count of the languages of other animals she knew. Then there was the shapeshifter language—full-body gestures, movement, and basic vocalizations, with different dialects for quadrupeds, birds, and other forms.

Sometimes, though, a person just had to scream.

"AAAAAAAAAAAAAAGH." The cry echoed around a small, empty antechamber and down the spiral stairwell leading from the room, furnishing the bare spaces with sound.

She sank to the checked marble floor, still naked, and lay on her back. Her brown hair flopped into her eyes; she attempted to blow it away once, twice, and gave up.

"Moss! Moooooss!"

After several interminable moments with nothing but echoes, she heard the faint zip of tiny wings. A jewel-blue hummingbird flew up the stairs and hovered over her, examining the burn marks. The hummingbird—Moss Growing in the Sunlight on a Boulder, Droplet's one remaining parent—fixed her with a disapproving glare and landed on the ground, the better to gesture.

Did you get cool water on it this time? Moss said in the language of shapeshifters.

"Yes," Droplet said in Makidan.

Good.

"I jumped in the sea to escape."

Moss sighed, a high, tinny noise when made by a hummingbird. She took back off and zoomed down the stairwell.

When Moss reappeared several minutes later, Droplet still had not moved. This time, Moss wore the form of a pale, gray-haired, wrinkled human, complete with a Makidan servant's uniform— loose white shirt, deep-green breeches—and a long-suffering expression. Though it was Moss's brains behind their operation, she posed as the butler here. She carried threadbare, stained towels, a bucket of water, and a basket of mashed paliot leaves, the best remedy for burns this side of the Kanian Sea.

"Who was the culprit this time?" Moss asked.

"Don't know," Droplet muttered. She continued lying on the floor as Moss began administering to the wound, though she hissed through her teeth at the initial, ice-like sting of crushed paliot on her burn.

"They got away, then."

"They did." Droplet fought to keep her voice steady. Moss had trusted her to handle this one alone, and she'd failed.

Moss patted her shoulder. "We can't succeed all the time. There's no shame in that," she said. Her words were warm, but the silence of the empty manor felt like an accusation. Back when they'd had the organization, no post-mission reunion was ever so quiet. Even on the failed nights, they'd wrap each other in chatter and bustle. Rangitam would get snacks for everyone. Yelarcha would interrogate the mission-goers on possible security breaches. And, on good nights, when Droplet or Moss or Moonshine had been on missions, they'd retell every detail in a mix of human, shapeshifter, and animal languages, shifting along with the tale in the way a human might gesture with their hands.

Now, only Moss and Droplet made up this shard of the fractured team. True, they could far-speak with the other survivors, scattered as they were, but it wasn't anywhere near the same.

"You know you'll need to keep one form for a few days so this can heal," Moss said.

"I'll do my best," Droplet said, because that technically wasn't a lie. "Could you bandage it?"

Moss obliged.

"Your mother would be proud of you," Moss said. The highest praise a shapeshifter could give. Rote words, but Moss said them sincerely. Droplet snorted in disbelief but didn't say anything. That was an old hurt, years old, and she didn't want to have that conversation again.

She moved at last, sitting up so Moss could wind the bandages around her chest.

"I did save some people tonight," Droplet said. "At least two. Maybe three. Probably not three."

Moss beamed, the smile sudden and warm. "Stop brooding, then!" she said, clapping Droplet on the back.

"Ow! I don't *brood*. I never *brood*. I'm exhausted, Moss."

"I'll toast you some bread, hm? You rest up. Not here. Get to your bed."

"Yes, thank you, yes," Droplet said, pushing herself up. Moss ruffled Droplet's hair, and Droplet let her with only the faintest grumble.

Droplet's bedroom was a floor above the antechamber, so she didn't have far to walk through the echoing, empty house before she collapsed onto the pile of furs that formed her bed. Later, jam-laden toast consumed, the burn soothed, Droplet still ruminated on the docks in a way that Moss probably would have described as brooding. The half-cat hybrid had tried to save her, no doubt about it, and Droplet had failed her. But she was gone now, wasn't she? Droplet created and discarded half a dozen plans to track down an invisible boat full of blood mages on the open ocean, plans that grew more absurd as she drifted toward sleep.

Half-dreamt plan number seven ("Recruit the whales...all of them... How many whales are there?") fled when footfalls pounded up the stairs. Human footsteps. She scrambled to all fours, ready to shift at a moment's notice. Stairs waged war against the human body. Moss running to her was bad; Moss running as a human was even worse. With the whole panoply of animal life available, no-body would willingly choose to run up stairs as a human.

Moss barged into Droplet's room flushed with exertion.

"What's happened?" Droplet asked.

"There's a human here," Moss gasped.

"At this hour?"

"That's what I said when she arrived. She was banging on the door—I had to see what the racket was. She says she has to speak with the lady of the manor, urgently, and she said..." Moss gulped for air. "She said, 'I'll see her in any form she wants.'"

"Stars. And it's just her? Nobody else?"

"Nobody that I could tell," Moss said, gesturing to her face. Human senses could miss a lot.

They'd been so careful with this manor and these identities. Moss had been crafting human personas and conning the wealthy for decades—gods knew she was meticulous at setting up a human identity. Had Droplet done something wrong? Droplet had only a few years of practice acting like nobility, and Moss had always joined her in the noble role before.

Maybe the human was bluffing. With a very specific bluff.

Only one way to find out, unfortunately.

"Do you feel well enough for this? I can always tell her the lady is indisposed," Moss said.

"Right, nothing suspicious about that," Droplet said sarcastically. Then, sincere, "I can do it, Moss. I can shift."

"I'm sorry to ask you. I would do it if I had the form."

"I know. Can you help me with the bandages?" said Droplet.

One shift later—her burned chest searing again as it reshaped, as if to say *Really?*—Droplet became Lady Kivak, enterprising Nortakian investor. She used her first human form for this role, one with waves of dark-brown hair and brown skin around the middle of the human spectrum.

Droplet dressed to intimidate in a long black robe with bespelled embroidery that flickered like flames across the fabric. The organization had bought houses for less money than this robe had cost; Nedrud was still, months later, teasing them about the expense during their far-speak talks. But, as Droplet had said darkly, few other people needed the organization's money these days. Only after buying the gown did Moss and Droplet learn that this style of robe was a Makidan dressing gown. Nedrud was going to be cracking jokes about it on his deathbed. But surely a wealthy Makidan human, dragged from their bed, would don something like this. *So there, Nedrud.*

Stars, she wished that bear was here right now.

"Where'd you leave the visitor?" Droplet asked.

"Outside the front door."

"Good."

"It doesn't look right, leaving a guest outside. One of these days, we do need to have at least one more person to handle these sorts of things."

If not for Droplet, Moss would have started recruiting new organization members years ago. But Moss kept telling Droplet she was an equal partner in this group, now, and that anyone who joined them needed to be someone they both trusted. Droplet hated the kindness and tenderness in Moss's voice when she talked about that, as if Droplet was a cub with a thorn in her paw and didn't understand why her parent kept tugging on the thorn when that only made it hurt more.

So Droplet didn't talk about it. "One day," she said, meaning *probably never.*

The front hall of the manor stretched two stories tall, stucco walls lit by bespelled crystals set in sconces of wrought iron leaves. A scattering of Nortakian wood carvings and tapestries adorned the walls, in hopes that wealthy visitors would be less likely to spot any glaring fashion faux pas in foreign art.

To keep up the illusion of nobility, Droplet stood back from the double doors as Moss tugged open the right-hand one. The door groaned. Droplet put on her best haughty expression.

In the doorway stood one of the most bedraggled humans she'd ever seen.

The human had been running. Moss had said "she"—yes, there, the human had the Sea Goddess's waves tattooed on one wrist. Her long black hair must have started out in a ponytail, but the tie had slipped most of the way down its length. Sweat beaded on her brown skin and soaked through the neck of her shirt—Droplet thought that type of loose, undyed, sleeveless shirt usually belonged to non-magical laborers, and the human's muscular arms backed that up. The human walked into the light of the manor without hesitation, meeting Droplet's assessing gaze with puffy, pleading eyes.

Tear tracks ran over her prominent cheekbones, smeared as though she'd tried to wipe them away at the last minute. "I need your help," she said.

"Who are you?" asked Droplet.

"Azera. Azera Carpenter. They took my friend. I need you to help me get her back."

"I don't know what you're talking about," Droplet said.

Azera took a deep breath. "I know you're a shapeshifter. I'm sorry to be so blunt about it. But we have to skip the part where you deny it, and I keep pressing the point, and you come up with flimsy reasons why you couldn't possibly have been the shapeshifter who fought on the docks tonight. Okay? There's no time for that."

Droplet took a much longer look at the human, hair to shoes. She felt boxed in, cornered, by a single magicless human a head shorter than her current form. But her mother and Moss, for all their disagreements, had both raised her to never let a human see her sweat, and she would be cursed if she started now.

Vows and righteous indignation aside, though, that pause in conversation was as good as a yes. No way around that. Ignoring Moss's gestures behind the human's back, Droplet said, "Fine, we can skip that part. Saves time for everyone. But why do you need my help, and why do you think I would help you?"

The human's face flickered with a brief smile of satisfaction, only there for a moment before grief, determination, and desperation swallowed it. "My friend is the one who charged down the dock after you. They got her," Azera said. Though Droplet had known that was the likely outcome of the hybrid's desperate charge, the words still came as a blow. "I don't know where they've taken her, or why, or what they're doing..." She took a deep, shuddering breath and clenched her fists. "You got the other people out of there. I figured you were a helpful sort of person."

"I don't know any more than you do about where they went," Droplet said, attempting to make her voice kinder this time. "It's not like the bastards left behind directions." Maybe she was out of practice with this "kindness" thing. "I don't know what stories they tell about shapeshifters in this city, but I can't track people over water, especially when they're in an invisible boat." She neglected to mention the hours she'd spent trying to solve this herself.

"You haven't given up, have you?" asked the human, surprised.

"No," Droplet retorted without conscious thought.

"Look, we can put our heads together, think up something. Maybe I can help. But I can't get my friend back alone. I need her back," Azera said.

"And you don't have any of your fellow humans to ask?" Droplet asked.

"No," the human said quietly. Droplet paused. She looked at Moss, who was speaking shapeshifter as best she could without alerting the human—moving her arms and hands in wide, slow motions, tilting her body, contorting her face to mimic growls and squeaks she couldn't utter. Droplet could understand the gist of it.

Hear her out.

Droplet wasn't about to trust a stranger again, let alone a human. She'd made that mistake before, and too many people had paid for it.

But Droplet wanted to save people. The human—Azera?—had gotten that right about her. And Droplet wanted to save the babbling cat who had tried to take on her captors with a broken crate. Needed to. If Droplet had been quicker, maybe she could have...but no, no use dwelling on that anymore. Time to see what this human could bring.

She nodded at Moss.

Moss stepped smoothly into Azera's line of vision and said, "Well, I'm Moss Growing in the Sunlight on a Boulder, but you can call me Moss. It's a pleasure to meet you, though what a shame it's under such circumstances. I'll get you both some tea. Why don't you sit down?"

Azera stared.

Moss bustled toward the kitchen.

Droplet gestured off the entranceway toward a sitting room.

Before following Droplet's gesture, the human asked, "So she's Moss. What's your name?"

I don't have one yet, Droplet thought. But saying that would only lead to more questions when she was dealing with a human. "Call me Droplet. Have a seat. And tell me everything."

Azera sat as far forward on the floral-patterned couch as possible, as if at any moment all of them would sprint after the blood mages on foot. On a better day, Droplet would have mimicked her pose, unwilling to let a human show more readiness than her. But the burns and the fight had taken their toll. Begrudgingly, she leaned back on her own couch, sinking into the fabric. She had to give humans credit for the invention of upholstery; she especially appreciated the luxury of being surrounded by cushioning at times like this, when so much of her ached.

Azera occasionally opened and closed her mouth, as if she was thinking of things to say and then reconsidering. That seemed more likely than that she was impersonating a fish. Her thoughts never became words, and Droplet and Azera waited in silence until Moss returned. Moss served the tea to Azera with the same encouraging smile she had used on Droplet in her childhood. After a few sips of tea, in fits and starts, Azera told her story.

"My friend is named Harra, Harra Virridaughter. She's part of one of the big half-cat clans in the city. We grew up together. We..." A sob bubbled up; she took a gulp of tea. "We went out to a pub tonight. We shouldn't have gone—we'd heard the rumors about people like Harra disappearing, but I'd just—well, anyway, we needed a drink. We were a few drinks in, she went to the water closet, and gods help me, it took me so long to realize something was wrong."

The human hesitated, brow furrowed in concentration. Putting together disjointed, tipsy memories? Planning a lie?

"I had some idea what could have happened to her once I figured out she was gone. I saw what happened at the docks from a distance—I didn't get there in time." This summary raised more questions than it answered, but Droplet was willing to overlook those for now.

"What did you see once I'd jumped off the dock?" Droplet asked.

"They grabbed Harra, and they pulled her and the cart into...well, it looked like thin air. Bloody perfect illusion."

"And then they were gone?" said Droplet.

"And then they were gone."

Droplet bit back her immediate response—to wonder how any of this information was helpful.

"Did you get a good look at them?" Azera continued.

"Can't say that I did," said Droplet. "A human and a raptor, and at least one was a blood mage—too powerful to be anything else. That's all I could tell while they were shooting things at me. They had the street sweepers' symbol on their tarp, though. Does that help?"

Azera's eyes went wide.

"Ah, so it does. Sudden fear is always a great sign," Droplet said.

"You're new here, aren't you?" Azera asked. Droplet grimaced. "Half the city is convinced the street sweepers are a cover for the Cult of the Endless War."

Droplet nearly dropped her tea.

"As you said. Always a great sign," said Moss.

Chapter Three

On the day young Droplet first encountered the Cult of the Endless War, she had gone into the human town of Bramblebreak to request some pies. A shapeshifter in her little colony had given birth that month, an occasion for wild and raucous celebration. Shapeshifters usually bore only one child in their life, so a moon after each child was born, shapeshifter communities marked the birth with two full days and nights of feasting, storytelling, singing, and general carrying-on. For a half-century or so, no birth celebration had been complete without the Jattarin family's pies, widely considered the best pies in the whole Pinewild mountain range.

Droplet practically strutted up the mountainside after she'd received this responsibility. She was young, after all, and up 'til that day, the older shapeshifters had insisted on accompanying her for any trading with the humans. Droplet was sure this mission meant the colony members were finally seeing her as an adult. Someone who could be trusted. She couldn't wait to tell her human friends. Soon, she would be able to formally participate in the shapeshifters' sacred mission to collect knowledge of the world. Maybe she'd be allowed to take on one of her human friends' forms. Maybe soon, she could make the pilgrimage to the desert, share her memories with the Enduring Archive, and receive her real name.

The sun shone down, the first buds of spring were beginning to bloom, and the flocks of yellowcaps had returned from their winter migration down the mountain.

Truly a promising day.

She found Alvar Jattarin, current head of the family business, alone in vis bakery. She'd never seen it empty before.

"Thank goodness! A customer," Alvar said. Ve whipped out an apron, peering at Droplet. "One of the Tinderfoot relatives from over the mountain? You've got the Tinderfoot chin...no, no, you're one of the shifters, aren't you?"

"I'm the older droplet," Droplet said. She was one of two droplets in her colony too young to have made the name pilgrimage. Her one human form did resemble a good many of the human families in town—her colony had been honoring people in the area for generations. Droplet's mother had told her stories of the people whose blood she'd inherited, from humans to cows to squirrels. Alvar's own mother was one of them, though Droplet didn't resemble Alvar or vis mother much, with their pointy noses and round faces. Droplet asked, "Are people not buying your bread? It's the best!"

"No, we're not short on coin, nothing like that. I just need an excuse not to leave the house today," Alvar grumbled. "Some wandering preacher came to town, and everyone's telling me I have to go see him."

Droplet made sympathetic noises. Most Makidans worshiped the same gods as shapeshifters, the First Four: the Goddess of the Sea, the God of the Earth, the Deity of the Air, and the Deity of the Rivers, with occasional nods to their dozens of offspring. Divine allegiance affected basic functions like gender, pronouns of address, styles of hair and clothing, and even some jobs worshippers were allowed to take—but as far as Droplet could tell, once someone selected a patron deity and got their tattoo, they didn't really *think* about them much. Alvar had a cloud tattoo, marking vim as someone sworn to the Air Deity, but had never spoken about gods before in Droplet's hearing.

"Is the preacher telling everyone to spend more time praying to the First Four?" Droplet asked.

"First Four? No, child, this man is here trying to preach about the guardians. Guardians, can you imagine it? The nerve of him."

Droplet didn't know why it took nerve to talk about the guardians. Her colony told stories about them now and then. But to be polite, she nodded.

Once she had placed the pie order, she searched for her friends. She didn't need to rush back to the colony. The celebration wasn't for a few days; there was plenty of time left for a young shapeshifter to socialize. Maybe show off to her friends a bit, too, coming to town alone and all. Humans grew up faster than shapeshifters did, and a couple of her friends had never stopped lording it over her that *they* could wander town alone and *she* couldn't.

After a few minutes of searching, though, she concluded that the most efficient way to find her friends would be to find this preacher everyone was seeing. Surely she could pry her friends away from that.

She headed for town square.

The preacher, a tall, thin man with only a hint of gray in his black hair, paced around the town's main well. A clever location for commanding interest—scattered among the listeners who wanted to take in some theology, other humans stood awkwardly holding buckets and pitchers. They didn't want to interrupt. All the mountain humans were painfully polite that way.

The preacher gestured so wildly as he paced that Droplet spent several minutes trying to read his movements in the shapeshifter language. He spoke with the ringing tones of someone convinced of their self-righteousness, and the crowd left a wide circle around him. Nobody wanted to catch his eye, not even the humans leaning in like they were watching for shooting stars. Droplet circled the crowd's edge, looking for her friends.

"Now preachers, they like to say the guardians abandoned us

even before they abandoned the raptors. But that's not true."

Droplet spotted one of her friends, Barch, and squirmed into the crowd, winding around the adults' legs.

"The guardians built our homes. Shared our meals. Blessed our children. Even the raptors tell the story of the guardian Harchieru and the children of Zadra, don't they?" Droplet had no idea who or what Zadra was, but apparently the humans did, because some were nodding thoughtfully. She reached Barch, a timid child who held his father's hand as they stood in the crowd. Although Barch waved at Droplet, when she tried to beckon him away, he shook his head as vigorously as a dog trying to dry itself and clutched his father's hand tighter.

"The guardians aren't coming back," a crowd member heckled the preacher. "They gave up on raptors, and serves those feathery lizards right."

Murmurs of assent rippled through the crowd. Droplet nodded along, pleased to know what people were talking about. The age of the guardians had ended a long time ago. The guardians had saved the world from destruction caused, in the "moral responsibility" sense, by the arrogance of raptors, but also caused, in the physical sense, by ravenous demons from another world. After defeating the demons, the guardians left the world behind as punishment for the raptor's arrogance.

Barch was a lost cause. Droplet looked for another friend.

The speaker on the well didn't seem perturbed by the crowd's objections.

"My friends, the guardians didn't want to leave. The guardians are still out there fighting for us, past the boundaries of the world we know."

"Fighting who?" scoffed a neman—a human sworn to the River Deity.

"The demons."

Droplet expected the crowd member to keep laughing, but ne

fell silent. Behind her, Barch gasped in fear, and she resolved that *she* wouldn't be afraid of any demons like that. *She* was practically a grown-up.

"The demons are dead," a woman said. "The guardians killed them, and good riddance."

"The raptors lied to us. Shocking, I know, raptors lying," he added. Some people in the crowd laughed, but their neighbors quickly shushed them. "It's not the guardians who abandoned us—it's the raptors. They wanted the guardians gone because they couldn't stand anyone more powerful than them."

On the other side of the crowd, a couple of Droplet's older friends whispered together. Perfect. Droplet wound her way through people's legs. If humans weren't such sticklers about clothes, she could have shifted and gotten over there so quickly! People were weird.

"If the raptors could get rid of guardians, then who needs guardians?" said a woman. "We have our gods, and the raptors can't do anything about that."

"But does the One of the Earth ever talk to you? Does the River Deity ever stop in for a mug of cider on a cold night? This is what the guardians did for us, back when they walked among us. They were more than gods—they were friends, protectors, companions."

"Sir, this is all fascinating, and I don't mean to be rude, but I need to get some water for my goats," said a villager.

The preacher looked at the well with wide eyes as if he'd never noticed it. "Of course, of course! My mistake—let me get out of your way..." ...and the spell seemed to break. Contemplation of the divine made way for the necessities of daily life. The preacher helped lower buckets and clasped shoulders with those who came up—a typical mountain greeting. Droplet had to dodge through the now-mobile crowd to get to her friends.

"Droplet! Perfect! We need more people for stickball," said one friend, Carn, a neling. Ne craned ner neck to look through the crowd. "Where's your mom? We'll tell her we've got you."

"I'm here alone," Droplet said, attempting to look five inches taller than she was.

"No way!" said the other friend, Marnil, a boy. He clapped her on the shoulder. "Great job, pipsqueak."

"I'm older than you!" Droplet said indignantly.

"Not by shapeshifter reckoning," said Marnil smugly. Maybe Droplet's mom was right about not telling shapeshifter secrets to outsiders. Centuries too late to fix that now, with this village and these humans.

After two raucous games of stickball, and after shaking off some of the ensuing dirt and mud, Droplet bid her friends goodbye, shifted into an eagle, picked her human clothes up in her talons, and headed home. She had mushrooms and nuts to gather, starbark to carve, recitations to memorize…a new baby took a lot of work from everyone.

When Droplet came back to Bramblebreak for the completed pie order a few days later, she almost didn't recognize the town. Strips of knotted cloth hung from half the doors. Words were scrawled in the dirt of the streets. People moved in clusters, some talking too loud with faces full of wonder, and some huddling, whispering, keeping their heads down.

No cloth knot hung on the Jattarin bakery's door, and someone had swept the dirt in front of it smooth, as if erasing scrawled words. When Droplet pushed the door open, Alvar jumped.

"Honored Jattarin, what happened to the town?" Droplet said.

"What happened? That preacher happened," Alvar snapped. "Me and my family, we've all followed the First Four for generation after generation, and they've done well by us. Everyone's got their gods in this town. But some smooth-talking stranger comes along yapping about flea-ridden, good-for-nothing guardians, saying they were really our friends all along—bloody nonsense, I tell you."

Ve kept up a similar string of invective as ve bundled up the pies. Droplet quashed her curiosity, didn't ask questions, and (after a brief discussion of logistics) became a mountain goat. Alvar secured the pie boxes to her, and she headed back down the mountain to home.

Weird things are happening in Bramblebreak, Droplet said to her mother after the pies were unloaded. A Bird That Chases Summer Around the World—Summerbird, for short—made a polite noise of interest. Droplet described what she'd seen. As soon as she got to the words written in dirt, though, her mother shrieked and changed from a lemur into a bear, crushing the branch she'd been sitting on and dropping to the ground.

Mom—

Don't! Silence! Into the bone pit! Droplet's mother emphasized her sentence with a deep growl. Droplet fled to the bone pit, her mother close behind. The pit, where the colony gathered bones from other animals' meals, was an effective magic cleanse, as inexorable as floodwaters over dirt. Still a goat, Droplet bounded into the pit. Summerbird used her claws to push rattling drifts of bones over her.

Mom, what is going on? Droplet said—or tried to say, as the combination of sounds and gestures in the shapeshifter language were difficult to convey while being buried under bones.

Lie down and hold still.

Droplet obeyed. Summerbird finished her impromptu burial. Droplet couldn't see, but she heard the soft, squishy noise of her mother shifting forms. Summerbird started talking in Makidan, the local humans' language, the language the preacher had used—and, critically, a language that did not require Droplet to see to understand. Droplet shifted to human, too, to respond. Bones slid and rattled around her as she shrunk.

"That preacher was part of the Cult of the Endless War. They lure humans in by telling them that those airheaded raptor guardians loved them. You know what humans are like when they hear someone loves them. The cultists gather a whole group of followers, and then, all together, the followers give their memories."

"What?! Like...like we do, with the Enduring Archive?"

"No, my droplet. They give their memories, and then they don't have them anymore. The priest doesn't have them either. They *say* the guardians have them, but that's a load of bat spit in my opinion. They're gone."

Droplet gasped. She couldn't help it. She knew humans didn't share their knowledge with all other humans, not the way shapeshifters did. But to destroy a memory?

Wait...

"They would have to give memories willingly, though, Mom. Right? For the magic to work. That's how other blood magic happens. So why do I have to sit in the bones?"

"The cultists know how to play herd animals like humans. They use their blood magic to ensnare two or three people. That's all they need. Once they have a few spelled followers saying, 'Oh, this is a good idea, let's hear them out,' others will follow."

"That's awful! We've got to stop them!"

"*No*, Droplet. You've already risked enough."

"But the village!" Droplet was shaking under the bones. She dug her fingers into the dirt, as much as she could with these useless human claws.

Her mother's tone turned soothing. "The villagers will survive, darling. You know human memories aren't like ours. They don't think of them like we do." Droplet couldn't argue with that. She'd grown up on hearing the usual shapeshifter stories, learning the heroes to emulate. Owl Eyes Under a Full Moon, whose memory of a late-blooming daffodil saved the colony from an avalanche. Glacier That Carves a Canyon, who tried for three years plus three moons to enter the raptors' Tower of Rahnor. The merry band of Roc Mountain shapeshifters who had mapped the land and then set off on a quest to map the ocean and one day—someday—would return to the shore.

Human heroes weren't like that, she thought. Her friends wouldn't know how important memories were.

"Can someone warn them?" Droplet pleaded.

"I'll tell the elders about this," Droplet's mother said. Droplet thought that meant yes. Still in that soothing tone, her mother continued, "You wait here. Even if the blood cultist used some magic on you, it will be cleansed soon."

"So you think the blood cultist decided to enchant me?" Droplet shivered under the cold bones. "Could...could he cast a spell on the pies too?"

"THE PIES!"

Years later, Droplet learned that she didn't know the whole truth of how blood magic worked. Every child was taught that blood magic only worked properly with a willing sacrifice—otherwise the spell warped and corrupted in ways even the best mages couldn't predict. Willing and unwilling sacrifices were as different as summer and winter, in magical theory. But in practice, the definition of "willing" could be stretched. Bent. Manipulated. Much like people, really.

When the days of festivities were over and most of the colony was still in a stupor from too much food and too little sleep, Droplet took to the skies and headed for Bramblebreak. The sun shone, and the buds had bloomed pink and white. Droplet caught a thermal, an updraft of sun-warmed air that lifted her into the sky. From high in the air, she observed the village, her eagle eyes catching even tiny details. Names still decorated the dirt, most of them names she knew. But people were walking around like normal—fetching water, herding animals in the common green, carrying children.

Heartened but still cautious, Droplet plunged downward. She surveyed the humans for several more minutes from the safety of the trees outside the village square. Yes, they still had the knotted strips of cloth on their doors. Something seemed off, too, in the faces of the villagers. Droplet moved from the tree to the ground and shifted again; she'd reached the limit of what eyesight could tell her. She became her human self and tied a wrap around her waist, just enough to be decent. She shivered a bit in the spring air.

Barch sat on a platform in a field of berry bushes near a row of houses. He was on crow-scare duty, then. Droplet walked up to him, waving. He eyed her suspiciously.

"Who are you?" he asked.

Droplet stopped, colder still than even the mountain air.

"You don't remember me?" she asked.

Barch looked guilty.

"You decided to forget me," Droplet said, and tears pricked in her eyes. That wouldn't do. That wouldn't do at all. She wouldn't let him see her cry. She stormed past him, past the line of houses and into the village proper, and became a dog.

The smell of blood surrounded her. Blood from the farrier, who had held the rope for skipping games. Blood from the thatcher, who had shown Droplet how to safely peel thornfruit. Blood from a man who sang midsummer songs all year round at the top of his lungs. They'd all given memories. What had they forgotten? Who had they forgotten? Old blood, old blood everywhere, in her nose no matter where she turned...

She fled down the mountain, tumbling tail over ears in her rush.

Chapter Four

Droplet and Moss interrogated Azera for almost an hour on how the Cult of the Endless War functioned in the city.

Rumors and folk wisdom built an incomplete picture. The cult did not have a base of power here in Ninuthen. Instead, members of the cult entered the city every few years to steal away sacrificial victims. They donned the clothing and emblems of the city's street sweepers to pass undetected. When they reached whatever arcane quota of victims their beliefs demanded, they vanished.

And that was it.

"We can work with this," Moss said with far more cheer than Droplet thought was warranted.

Moss had refreshed their cups with a sweeter tea minutes ago; Droplet took another sip and attempted to project calm authority, as if she knew exactly what Moss had in mind. She wanted to be alert and ready to go as soon as Moss shared her idea.

While Droplet drank, Moss continued, "We've made some contacts in the city who may know more."

Aha! Trust Moss to think of the radical strategy of "ask other people." Droplet knew where they stood now. She said to Azera, "Where should we find you for updates?"

"Wait, what?"

"I need some place to find you after we're done," Droplet said. She tried to keep her voice slow and patient. After all, the human had had a very trying evening.

"I'm coming with you," Azera said.

"What?"

"You think I'm trying to…to hire you for a job? Harra's my friend. I'm coming along, whatever you do."

"Absolutely not," Droplet said. "I had a hard enough time saving my own skin from these people. Saving your friend will be three times as hard. I haven't even done the math on trying to save someone else and myself while playing nursemaid to a magicless human."

"Calculate quickly. I'm not abandoning Harra—" Azera interrupted herself with a yawn, looking very startled about it.

"How will it help your friend if you"—Droplet yawned, too, but shook herself—"if you get yourself injured or killed? I…I…" She stopped to collect her thoughts, but instead she yawned again.

Azera didn't seem to notice. The human's eyelids fluttered, and she slumped backward into the couch, as if whatever force had held her awake was draining away.

Droplet had enough sense left to look accusingly at Moss, who was clearing up the empty teacups.

"Not *again*, Moss—" Another yawn stopped her. From her own couch, Azera made an indignant, incomprehensible series of sounds.

"Neither of you are in any shape to do more tonight."

"But the bad guys will get away," Droplet mumbled. Strange how the room was swaying like that…she felt upholstery cradle her cheek.

"Leave the rest of the night to me," Moss said, and that was the last thing Droplet heard before the drugged tea won.

The next morning, Droplet awoke in confusion on the sofa. She stared blankly at the worn wood rosettes of the sitting room ceiling. Why was she in the sitting room? Why had she slept in a human form, such a terrible body for getting a proper, comfortable

rest? Why was there a *human in the room oh stars*—
The world righted itself as memories of last night emerged from
the fog of early-morning thoughts.

Azera still slept on the opposite couch, face peaceful. Her hair
tumbled over her face, and she snored. Droplet stretched stiff
limbs, realized her extravagant dressing gown was falling off, and
wrapped it around herself. She thought she'd been quiet, but as
soon as she'd tied the robe shut, Azera began to stir.

Droplet sat up.

"Ah good, you're awake," said Moss.

Droplet turned to glare at her parent and mentor, who sat in a
chair, knitting.

"No thanks to you," Droplet said.

"If it weren't for me, you'd be falling asleep on a road sometime
around now from sheer exhaustion," Moss said matter-of-fact-
ly. This was not the first time Moss had ensured Droplet's well-
being whether the younger shapeshifter liked it or not. Droplet and
Azera both began angry retorts that did nothing to affect Moss's
placid, satisfied expression. She held up a hand. "I've been gathering information while you slept," Moss continued as if they hadn't
said anything. "I trust you'll be interested?"

Scowling, Droplet leaned against the back of the couch. Azera
crossed her arms, which made her look much younger, like a surly
child.

"Did you find out where Harra went?" Azera said.

"Yes." For the first time, Moss's placid exterior faltered. Like an
apology, she said, "She's in Sacarus."

"Sacarus. Stars," Droplet swore.

"The City of a Thousand Eyes? *That* Sacarus?" said Azera.

"That Sacarus," Moss said.

"Figures," Droplet said. "How did you find that out?"

"I visited half the stables around Ninuthen," Moss said.

"Ohhh, smart," Droplet said, seeing the connection instantly.

Azera looked baffled.

Moss saw the human's confusion too and, to Droplet's dismay, explained, "The garzis go everywhere, and they're much more reliable than human or raptor informants." The lanky, four-legged, long-necked, flightless birds pulled carriages and carried riders on their backs.

"Of course. Nobody would bother bribing a garzi to keep quiet," Azera said.

"And nobody would bother wiping their memory," said Droplet. Azera flinched. Moss frowned at Droplet, which seemed deeply unfair. What had Droplet done wrong? She needed the human to be aware of the dangers. How was now a time for tact?

But Droplet wasn't about to argue with her remaining parent in front of an outsider.

Moss went on, speaking to Azera, "Garzis don't have the same priorities as their riders, of course, so it can take quite some time to search this way. The fine young steed who helped me the most was baffled that I was interested in the magic his renter had used instead of the delicious roasted corn said renter had fed him."

Azera smiled for only a heartbeat, but her face seemed less pained even once the smile was gone.

"So they're definitely in Sacarus?" she asked.

"Yes, the garzis were quite consistent. Street sweepers take the garzis to Sacarus, often with crates of people."

"Where in Sacarus?" Droplet asked.

"Nobody knew."

"If the cultists stay in the city for more than a day, we have a chance," Azera said. "Did you find out anything about how long they meet?

"No, but the sacrifices seem to happen in summertime. Your friend mentioned midsummer, if I remember Droplet's report right. The shortest night is three nights away, yes? That's a powerful time," said Moss. Shapeshifters held a solemn ceremony on the shortest night to bring back the starry sky. Humans and raptors had their own midsummer celebrations, though Droplet was unclear on the purposes of their rituals. Their celebrations usually involved fireworks and lots of food, which described most human and raptor celebrations that Droplet was aware of, and she had never bothered keeping them straight.

"That doesn't leave us much time to spare," Droplet said to Moss. "Do you...? Will you...?" She didn't know what she wanted to ask. *Let me go, I can handle this,* or *Please go, please don't trust me with this.*

"I'll stay and prepare our story for Lady Kivak. We'll need one of us here to keep up the illusion. You can go after Harra," said Moss. Moss smiled at Droplet, warm and proud, and Droplet felt some of her fear melt in the face of that unspoken belief in her.

I can do this, Droplet thought. She turned to Azera.

"I don't know what stories you've heard about Sacarus. It does seem like you've heard the right *sort* of stories," Droplet said. Many spoke of Sacarus wistfully, wishing they could experience the private islands, each with painstakingly bespelled mansions. From as far away as the Iasnesh Empire, the elite of the world glided into exclusive parties on these islands, where magic and servants ensured the partygoers' every whim was satisfied. The guests departed with a library's worth of stories to spread...but so did the servants. "I promise, the real thing is even more sordid. It would be much better if I went alone." Droplet tried to seem stoic and composed and tried to not think about the ever-watchful Eyes of the city, and—in some ways, worse—the unfeeling eyes of the wealthy and powerful.

"If you try and leave without me, I'll go by myself," said Azera without any rancor. Just a statement of immutable fact, like describing the weather. "So. What's the quickest way to Sacarus?"

Chapter Five

Droplet had only five human forms, and one of those wasn't worth considering; she wouldn't honor that one with use. She decided to make the trip to Sacarus in the same human form she'd used when she first arrived home the night before. She used this form for trips to the city when she didn't want to play the part of a human of wealth and taste. When she'd taken on this man's form, he had already gotten the tattoo of three mountain peaks to show his allegiance to the Earth God. Tattoos came along with the form; therefore, Droplet would be posing as a man for this trip. Droplet occasionally made offerings to the Earth, River, and Air Deities as an apology for impersonating their followers; she also gave extra offerings to the Sea Goddess so she wouldn't get jealous.

She'd picked the name Dalere for this form, a common Makidan name. Azera didn't seem concerned at Droplet's use of multiple human forms; she must not know much about how shapeshifters worked. That was a relief.

Droplet and Moss kept a room full of clothes and other accessories for their many human guises. To Droplet's dismay, Moss offered Azera use of the supply room as well, to pack for the journey ahead. Droplet surveyed her options and selected quickly. Clothes were easy—she picked the same common, cheap clothes Azera wore.

Bones were harder. She reached out for a necklace of parrot wing bones, hesitated, reached for a turtle-skull necklace, hesitated again. She remembered the smell of blood all around her and reached for the most potent bone in their collection—a fragment of a dragon skull. Bones craved the life they once had, and a life as long as a dragon's left a yawning void of desire that guzzled up magic. Droplet tucked the dragon-bone necklace under her shirt with a sense of relief.

Droplet offered Azera the parrot wing-bone necklace, but Azera declined, saying she had her own. Droplet couldn't see one, but this wasn't unusual. Makidans were sensitive about bone charms. Mages in this country wielded the elements with impunity, yet were affronted, nay, aghast, that non-magical humans would want some guaranteed protection from errant floods and fireballs. Non-magical humans had devised a variety of ingenious ways to conceal their bone charms rather than inviting an upstanding magical citizen to ask, "Do you not *trust* us?"

Over a quick breakfast, Azera, Droplet, and Moss worked out a rudimentary backstory for why Dalere the Normal Human knew Azera, in case they ran into someone Azera knew: Dalere would be Azera's new apprentice.

"After all, everyone knows I'm desperate for money," Azera said, her voice overflowing with bitterness.

"*I* didn't know that," said Droplet. "Are there key parts of your personal history that I need to know before I take you with me?"

After a moment's pause, Azera squeezed her eyes shut and spoke. "Up until last week, I was engaged to marry a rich woman. Said woman ended our engagement. My family is not happy with me. That's all you need to know. Everything else is merely rampant speculation around town." Her voice wobbled, and she swallowed back a sob.

Droplet nodded. "Your first engagement?" she said.

Azera nodded.

"What a shame. My sympathies," Moss said.

Azera thanked Moss while Droplet mumbled some pleasantry. Unfortunately for Droplet, Azera's history didn't present any opportunities for a last-ditch effort at convincing the human to stay out of this quest for Harra's recovery. Makidans could bring as many partners as they wanted into their household, of any gender, so long as all existing partners in the household agreed. But Azera didn't have any partners to appeal to, and the "think of what your mother would say" tactic never worked as well with humans as with shapeshifters even at the best of times, let alone when the members of the human's family had fallen out.

"I have complete faith in you," Moss said to Droplet in a brief moment away from the human. Moss handed over the far-speak discs they'd be using to check in each day. "Rangitam knows you're coming, too. I managed to contact him last night." Another old organization member, Rangitam had found a home in Sacarus after they'd had to scatter.

"Good. Good. It'll be great to see him again. Nice to have...nice to have help," Droplet said. Here, with only Moss, she didn't bother hiding her nerves.

Moss embraced her. Droplet hugged back, nuzzling Moss's head. She didn't hug as a human often.

"Be safe, my child," said Moss.

The postal coach was the quickest transportation to Sacarus, and Azera and Droplet left for it as soon as they'd packed and eaten.

With Droplet's still-wounded chest, she would need to stay in human form for the whole walk to the postal-coach yard. It was, indeed, a walk; after all the information Moss had managed to glean from the garzis, neither of them felt inclined to rent birds for the journey.

They stepped out into a beautiful morning. Droplet gazed at the few white, fluffy clouds dotting the springtime sky and listened to the songbirds, more out of habit than from any expectation that they'd say anything useful. She settled into the long, easy strides of her human walking gait. When the actual human next to her talked, she nearly jumped out of her skin.

"So, tell me more about yourself," said Azera.

Droplet looked down at her. "Why?"

"Well, we can't make the whole trip to Sacarus in silence, can we? We'll sink so far into our own heads that we'll only be able to talk in glowers and grunts."

"Glowers and grunts can take you far in life," Droplet said.

Azera smiled hesitantly; she looked as if she wasn't sure whether that had been a joke. "I just figure we should get to know each other if we're going to be spending time together," Azera said.

Droplet raised one eyebrow, attempting to channel skepticism in its purest, most potent form. She was glad she'd chosen a taller human form for the trip.

Azera sighed and turned back to the road.

Silence reigned for several minutes as the tree-shaded, hedge-lined roads of the wealthy narrowed, and the buildings grew smaller and squeezed together.

Droplet would be stuck with this human for several days. At least Azera didn't seem half bad, really. Passionate, determined, and she cared for at least one non-human in the world. That was more than most humans could say. But that was the problem, wasn't it? If Droplet thought a human's care extended farther than their fingertips, she'd only get burned. And "getting to know" a human...Droplet mentally surveyed that narrow, swaying, rickety bridge, and decided she'd cross it again only if she had to.

But Azera could be useful, even if she couldn't be a real partner in the mission.

"How about you tell me about Harra?" Droplet asked. "You can talk, I can glower and grunt, and we'll both be happy."

"Harra's my best friend," Azera said without hesitation. "She walked up to me in school, maybe eight years old, while I was in the middle of reading *The Haunting Tribulations of Marb*, and told me I'd be happier with another book. When I said she was being very rude, she tried to convince me by telling me the ending."

Droplet snorted. "That's one of those Upright Mages' Collective books, right?" The Upright Mages' Collective churned out an absurd number of didactic, moralistic books for children, their titles as formulaic as everything else about them. Droplet wasn't much for reading, but even she knew the gist: plucky young person with old-fashioned name learns to stand up to an anti-magic crusader, or a necromancer, or a bully, by using such innovative strategies as "saying no" and "telling a mage"—or does *not* stand up to the adversary and comes to a tragic end.

"So you see, Harra was right, but was I, also eight, about to admit that? No. Clearly I hadn't read enough books by the Upright Mages' Collective," she said. Droplet couldn't help a smile at that, and Azera grinned in return as though she'd won a game Droplet hadn't known they were playing. "A week or so later, once a teacher had sat me and Harra down for a nice chat about how to properly share hobbies with others, Harra started smuggling me decent books. Kept it up all the way until I had my own money to sneak books." Azera's eyes were growing watery, although she still smiled.

"A good friend," Droplet said.

Azera continued talking about Harra—her giant family, her love of upper-crust gossip, her impeccable fashion sense—until she burst into full-on sobs in the middle of a bustling market street. Droplet silently dug out a handkerchief from her travel pack and handed it to Azera to dry her eyes and blow her nose. Droplet didn't know how to comfort her, and the only strategies she could think of were platitudes like "We'll get her back." How could Droplet promise that? Instead, she led the human onward, glaring at the shoppers and vendors whose gazes lingered on them.

Once she'd finished crying, Azera took a deep, deep breath, then smoothed her face into serenity with the skill of a professional actor. Droplet's skin crawled seeing the change.

"Sorry. I needed that cry," Azera said.

"You have nothing to apologize for," Droplet said. *Although if you could explain your uncanny acting ability, that would be nice.*

But Droplet said nothing more, and Azera didn't explain. Instead, they walked in silence for rest of the trip to the mail coach.

Chapter Six

Soon after arriving at the mail coach, Droplet learned that she and Azera had very different approaches to public transportation.

Droplet's typical strategy was to give her fellow passengers the courtesy of her indifference and silence. She expected them to give her the same. Thus their lives, though in forced proximity, could carry on undisturbed as they passed through time and space.

Azera made small talk.

Even that could have been bearable had there not been a local leverball game the night before. The team from Azera's neighborhood, Carver's Row, had played their hated, eternal rivals, Riverside. As luck would have it, one of the mail-coach passengers, a tawny-feathered raptor, wore a blue Riverside charm in his crown-feathers next to the mountain sigil that marked him for the Earth God. Azera and the raptor were soon trading cheerful insults about the ability, appearance, moral fortitude, and parentage of the opposing team's supporters.

When the time came for the coach to leave, Azera sat on the creaking wooden bench next to Droplet, and the new sports rival sat directly across from Azera. Apparently, these kinds of insults led to something similar to friendliness. A few other passengers took up most of the remaining space on the open top of the coach.

"So what's bringing you north on this lovely day?" Sports Man asked, gesturing to Azera and Droplet. Droplet leaned into the conversation casually, just like a real human who wasn't hiding anything about their normal, ordinary trip to a notorious city.

Azera took the lead in responding. "We're going to find a friend of mine. She got suckered into one of those get-rich-quick schemes...you know how they go."

"I thought everyone did," Sports Man said. "What, a wealthy Nortakian clan leader needed someone to hold his money? A dragon needed some kind souls to help count its vast hoard of gold?"

"To be fair to her, the offer was more plausible than most. Help needed for a midsummer party at one of the richest little Sacarian islands...last-minute, but the pay sounded great. Way better than the house she was working at. Anyway, she headed north, and now she's stuck in Sacarus without a job and without money to get back." Droplet, Azera, and Moss had come up with the alibi together, spun from the true fact that Harra worked as a maid in a noble house.

"My sympathies." Sports Man held out his hand to Azera. He hadn't capped his claws, Droplet noted, which was unusual. Raptors tended to cover their claws here in Makido, in deference to the ruling humans. "I don't think we've been introduced. I'm Solvim."

"Azera," the human said, shaking his hand.

"Dalere," Droplet said, shaking his hand in turn. "I'm the bodyguard."

The human form she'd taken for Dalere was on the slighter side, but Droplet knew how to carry herself. Solvim didn't question it. "Impressive that you'd sign on for this trip. Sacarus is not for the fainthearted."

"Oh, Dalere is anything but that," Azera said, "and he's been to the city before."

Droplet wished she could tell Azera "Don't offer details you don't have to," but the human wouldn't recognize shapeshifter speak.

"What's your story?" Droplet asked the man instead.

"Oh, me? I'm a wanderer," Solvim said, leaning back and gesturing expansively—or as expansively as he could without knocking over Azera and the passenger to his left. "I've been all over the old

Empire lands." Everything between the mountains and the seas, then. Droplet relaxed again. She knew this kind of person, raptor or human. Start one of them talking about their travels, and nothing short of a rain of fireballs would stop them from rhapsodizing about the views they'd seen from the peak of Mount Kahessa or improvising a soliloquy about a little village in North Ganlia where barefoot beggar children taught them the true meaning of magic.

Droplet made an encouraging noise after half a minute of the elegy. At the next pause in conversation, Azera made an identical noise; Solvim took it as permission to continue. Azera caught Droplet's eye and grinned; Droplet found herself smiling back. At the next pause, she ventured an "Interesting." Azera took the next pause, with "Go on." As the tight-packed buildings of Ninuthen gave way to open spaces, the human and shapeshifter passed the conversation back and forth between them until Azera got bored and started asking pointier and pointier questions.

"But how do you *pay* for things on the road?" she finally asked.

"I take odd jobs here and there. You'd be amazed how much simple work there is across the continent. That's where you meet the real, honest, humble people, you know. Here in Ninuthen, I always find a place with the street sweepers."

Droplet fell back on her original noise of mild interest to cover up her shock. Azera's eyes and mouth went wide for only a moment. By the time Solvim had finished telling them about the time he'd harvested saltmelons on the edges of the Tatterhorn, Azera had composed herself enough to nod politely. Droplet controlled her facial features as her mind whirred.

How to probe him for information without tipping him off?

Unfortunately, before she could figure out any line of useful-yet-subtle inquiry, someone else on the cart broke out a deck of cards. After a few hands of towerfall, the raptor who had lost the most money called for a turn to storytelling, and an old neman obliged. The tale was common and predictable: a young human mage used cunning and cleverness to save a kingdom from a necromancer. Droplet tuned it out and turned over one plan after another for how to deal with the probable cultist. She hoped Azera was doing the same.

The coach stopped for the night at a town that existed to be a resting point between larger, more interesting towns. Droplet and Azera's mail coach was one of many in the coach yard, and the stables held dozens of garzis. The stables smelled of clean straw bedding, plentiful feed, and well-groomed birds. A couple of plump cats lazed on hay bales, glowering at the crowds.

No doubt most of the travelers would be heading to Sacarus to enjoy the solstice festivities. Droplet booked a single room for the night for Azera and herself. Fortunately for Droplet's purse, most Makidans took the view that adults willing to put up with each other's snores could share rooms and beds in whatever gender combinations they wished, with no scandal attached.

Their ground-floor room had a properly locking door and looked out into the stable yard. The aroma of clean straw mostly covered up the smell of manure. Once Azera lit the lantern, illuminating the off-white walls and wooden beams, the space seemed positively homey. Perhaps not the most thematically appropriate place to be discussing the immediate threat of a blood mage, but Droplet wouldn't complain about the comfort. She shucked off her shirt so she could smear more of Moss's crushed paliot leaves on her burn. Thanks to the ointment, the burn was healing fast, but it was still sore.

"If Solvim's a cultist, he must know where Harra's gone," Azera said.

"Midsummer's in two days. Surely all the cultists know where they're meeting by now," Droplet agreed. Even basic elemental light and air magic could make a far-speak charm—with blood magic at their disposal, the cultists would have no excuse for poor communication. "If you lure him out back, 1 can try to knock him unconscious... Would the inn have a bone store we could use?"

Azera looked at Droplet as though she was speaking Nortakian. "Why would we attack him? He loves to talk. All we need to do is get out there and keep him talking."

"And how do you recommend we get him to talk about his secret blood cult?" Droplet asked.

"Pretend to be interested converts? Ask about his hobbies? Get into a debate about the best calendrical system?" She smiled and gestured wide, tilting her hands and head.

Droplet spent several moments puzzling over why Azera said **The area before us is bountiful and you feast on rotten fish** before remembering that the human didn't know the shapeshifter language. Droplet shook herself. *Ignore the human gestures.* Aloud, she admitted, "Subterfuge isn't one of my strengths." Moss and Nedrud both excelled at leading conversations, as did other allies of the organization. Not for the first time, Droplet regretted the years she had spent convinced that all she needed to conduct proper rescue work was fast reflexes, good shifting, and courage.

"You're literally posing as a wealthy human businessperson, back home. What do you think that is?"

"That's *easy* subterfuge. Every rich human thinks they're better than all the other rich humans in the room. 1 know I'm better than all the rich humans. Nobody suspects a thing."

Azera laughed genuinely from her belly. Maybe Droplet was wittier than she gave herself credit for. When Azera had stopped laughing, she said, "Sorry, it's just...1 spent a lot of time with nobles in the past year, and 1 needed to hear that. So. 1 can talk to Solvim. Couldn't you shapeshift into something stealthy to eavesdrop? Like a rat?"

"Everything tries to kill rats," Droplet said. "One moment of inattention and bam, a cat has you in its paws."

"Why don't you tell it you're a shapeshifter?"

"Oh, like a cat's never heard that before. 'Please, your whisker-ness, if you move your claws, I'll show you...'"

Azera stared. "Rats can do that?"

"Oh yeah. Imaginative sorts, rats. Almost as good as magpies at spinning tales."

"And we kill them," Azera said to herself, aghast.

Droplet brightened. Maybe this human wasn't hopeless. "You do! And you humans don't even have the common decency to eat them after."

Azera stared at Droplet. Droplet stared back, riffling through her mental notes on Makidan customs. What had she said wrong?

"I think after this is over, I'd love to have some conversations with you about what 'common decency' means to a shapeshifter," Azera said. "But back to Solvim..."

They kept tabs on the inn's common room through the mundane solution of cracking the door and peeking out every few minutes. Droplet activated the far-speak disc to check in with Moss, who had no new information for them but approved the plan and gave them rousing encouragement. The smells of roasting chicken and simmering stew wafted in from the doorway, and soon, both Droplet and Azera's stomachs growled. Once Solvim had emerged from his room and taken a seat, the human and shapeshifter went out to join the crowd. Droplet's heart raced like a hummingbird's.

As they'd suspected, Solvim waved them over. He'd sat at one end of a long wooden table. Azera and Droplet took seats across from him on the well-polished bench.

The human and raptor took up idle chitchat without a snag, as if there had been no interruption in their pleasantries since the cart.

"The rooms are nice, aren't they?" said Azera.

"They're splendid! These coaching inns are so well kept. Not like some places you find on the road," said Solvim.

"Dinner smells great. I'm starving," said Azera.

Solvim exclaimed, "You *must* let me tell you about this one dinner I had at the foot of Mount Hokkarik. I'd been trekking through the singing pines for hours when I came across a family of Tangar nomads and their scalehounds..."

Droplet told herself that at least the all-encompassing boredom was suppressing the terror. By the time they'd gotten food—two-bean stew for her, chicken pies for Azera and Solvim—she was breathing easy again.

"Do you always travel alone?" Azera said, stabbing the question into a slight pause in yet another tale of Solvim's great adventures. She shivered, so quick Droplet almost missed it.

"Not at all! I'm actually meeting some friends. They should be here any moment now—I'll introduce you."

"Any moment?" Droplet said, puzzled. How would he know that? Azera's face blanched. Goosebumps prickled on the human's skin.

"Oh, I...I heard their coach getting into the yard," Solvim said, as if anything could be heard from outside over the din of others eating, drinking, and carrying on.

Droplet counted on Azera to say something, but the human was silent. Before the pause could get awkward, though, the door to the inn swung open. The pressure on Droplet's skin changed, like the tension in the air when a thunderstorm approaches: the feeling of lingering magic.

When a mage—or an object, or a monster, or a plant—had wielded enough power, everyone could feel the warping of power in the air. Without saying a word, a strong mage announced their presence wherever they went, the aftereffects of their spellcasting radiating from them like heat.

And now six newcomers crowded into the inn, a mix of raptor and human. Solvim looked around at the sound of the creaking door and yelled "Hey!" over the tables. The newcomers yelled back

"Hey!" and variations thereof with equal enthusiasm. A boisterous crowd of blood mages came straight for Droplet and Azera's table. *Azera has good people skills. Surely she'll think of a way to get us out of this,* Droplet thought.

Five minutes later, still in her seat, surrounded by blood mages, Droplet realized that Azera may have been relying on *her* to get them out of this.

Oops.

Solvim introduced the group as "kindred spirits, fellow travelers. The new incarnation of the Folk of the Road." They had names that must have passed through Droplet's ears but could find no place to stick because Droplet was drawing on the experience of every lie she'd ever told to seem calm in the face of people who could, without question, kill her or worse. She was used to having the upper hand with humans and raptors. With so many blood mages around, Azera fidgeted in her seat, drumming her fingers on the underside of the table where the blood mages couldn't see them. She must have been more sensitive to the magic. Droplet liked the feel of magic in the air—it kept her alert.

"So why a trip to Sacarus, of all places?" asked one of the blood mages, a short raptor woman. She had black, iridescent feathers interspersed with patches of white, like a magpie. She sat awkwardly on these benches designed for human joints and did her best to keep her wicked-looking footclaws from scratching anyone.

"My friend fell for a scam. She's stuck there with no money, so I'm coming to help her afford the journey back," Azera said. Though she continued to fidget, her voice was natural, Droplet observed with some admiration. Not for the first time, she noted that Azera must have had a lot of practice lying, which, yes, raised some question about what kind of person Droplet was traveling with. But in the moment, Droplet wasn't about to complain.

The human man next to Azera lifted a hand as if to pat her on the shoulder. Droplet tensed every limb. She was ready to lunge and knock Azera away from him, stealth be cursed. She'd seen too well what a blood mage could do with a touch. But the man withdrew his hand halfway there as if reconsidering physical contact with total strangers. Droplet tried to command her muscles to untense. Shockingly, this did not work.

"You're a good friend," the man declared. He raised a tankard that was nearly empty despite the scarcity of minutes he'd had it. "May we all find friends as loyal as you."

A staggered chorus of "hear, hear" rang out around the table, with many accompanying tankards bobbing. Azera looked around, possibly for someone to bring her a drink, possibly for the nearest exit.

"Does this sort of thing happen often?" the magpie raptor asked. She hadn't raised her tankard for the toast. She didn't seem to have any blood handy. Hard to tell whether she had any scabs to conveniently pick under her downy finger-feathers. None of the raptors at the table had capped their claws, though, so blood could be drawn faster than a breath.

"Oh no, Harra's usually quite bright," Azera said, and at that, half the mages, including Solvim, stiffened. Azera faltered but tried to recover. "She works for a demanding household, and, uh, she was getting pretty desperate."

Why had they reacted to that? Droplet wondered. The story wasn't the most ironclad alibi imaginable, but intelligent people fell for scams all the time... Did the blood mages somehow know Harra's name? Not for the first time, she wished Azera knew shapeshifter language.

"A shame, what a shame," said the man with the tankard.

"Not Harra Virridaughter?" asked Solvim. The lively chatter of the inn couldn't cover up the sound of several people kicking him under the table nor hide the pained look he shot at his friends.

"No, sorry," Azera said, with slightly more presence of mind than Solvim.

"We should get back to the room, Azera," said Droplet. "You said you were going to write that letter to her parents."

Azera didn't miss a beat. "Of course. We should get that written before bed. It was lovely meeting you all," Azera said, standing up. They retreated at a nonchalant stroll, despite all of Droplet's senses screaming for her to run.

"Well that went poorly," Azera muttered once they'd reached the relative privacy of the room.

"You said her name?" Droplet hissed.

"How was I supposed to know cultists would know the name of one of their victims? What in the demon-blighted hells does that do for them?"

"I told you to stay home and let me handle this."

"Yeah, but that was never going to happen, so don't pull out an I-told-you-so voice."

"I did tell you so."

"It's not like you were any more help down there."

"I got us away, didn't I? After *someone* told everyone who we were looking for."

"Maybe they bought it when I said Harra's family name wasn't Virridaughter?" Azera said. Droplet gave Azera a look. "Yeah, yeah, I was being hopeful. I see you're not familiar with the concept."

"Hope doesn't get you anywhere."

"What the hells are you doing this for, then?"

"Because someone has to!" Droplet shouted. She clamped her mouth shut as if doing so could retroactively stop the noise. Surely the whole inn had heard that. Dropping back to a furious whisper, she added, "Because you don't need to have hope to do the right cursed thing anyway." She'd expected a glower, but Azera had softened. The human broke eye contact to look at the floor and scuffed the toe of her worn boot against the wood.

"That's good to hear," Azera said.

"What did I say?"

"Don't worry about it. You're right, you know. Whether or not there's any hope, we have to do this."

"Right."

"Right."

Droplet closed her eyes and attempted to calm her nerves through sheer determination. Like her muscles, her nerves failed to cooperate. Her stomach was in knots, though at least she wasn't hungry anymore.

"We can't pass up this chance to learn more. Let's go back to the eavesdropping idea," Droplet said.

"The one where you get eaten?" Azera said.

"We were thinking too small. I'll be a cat."

"This is a terrible idea," Azera said.

"Excuse me? You were all for it a few hours ago."

"That's when we had one blood mage to deal with, and a clueless one at that. Did you *feel* the magic in that room? Any one of them could crush us like mosquitoes. It's not worth it."

"We've got a whole city to search when we get to Sacarus, and Sacarus doesn't take kindly to people poking around its dark corners. Anything we can learn now will save us a world of pain later."

"And any pain we get now means even more pain later!"

"They might be coming for us anyway," Droplet pressed.

Azera's eyes widened. "Blood and bones. I hadn't thought of that," she said. They fell silent. Droplet walked to the window over the bed and tested the hinges. They creaked, but the window opened outwards. She shut it again, not latching it. Azera continued, "Then let's leave. Now. Rent a garzi—nobody else will be talking to them, not any of the blood mages anyway. Get as far as we can as fast as we can."

"I'm not leaving our only lead," Droplet snapped. "I've done this before, remember?"

"Nothing like this—not alone," Azera retorted. When Droplet gaped, Azera said, "You think I didn't hear what you and Moss said? Now, I don't know everything that's going on here," she said, gesturing toward Droplet, "but you don't act alone. You haven't gone running off solo into a nest of blood mages before, or I'll eat my shoe."

Droplet couldn't speak for a moment, heat flushing her face as she remembered the smell of blood, the blank face of a friend, and the twisted normalcy of a destroyed town. The triumph of a successful mission with a whole house full of companions, the smell of an inferno, and the sounds of cracking beams.

"You came to me," Droplet growled, wishing her human canines could extend into fangs, wishing Azera could see her hackles raised. "Let me do my job."

Azera took a step back and lifted her hands, palms up in surrender. "You know best, of course," she said, and Droplet chose to ignore the bitterness in her voice. Her opinion didn't matter.

Chapter Seven

Soon after the cult took over Bramblebreak, Droplet's mother decided she and Droplet would travel to the city of Panithen, at the southern border of Makido, to spend time with Moss Growing in the Sunlight on a Boulder.

Moss was Droplet's other biological parent, but more importantly, in shapeshifter eyes, Moss was an old friend of Summerbird's. Young Droplet had spent her whole life hearing how she clearly had Moss's blood. Moss herself had stayed with the colony many times over the years. But Moss, more and more frequently, had chosen to spend her time among the arrogant animals—the humans, the raptors, the ones that saw themselves as better than other species. (Summerbird usually tackled colony members who sneered about this. They were a very direct colony.)

Droplet felt as though her heart would burst from anticipation the whole trip. Summerbird had raised her like a proper shapeshifter, with plenty of exploration to discover the world around her. Droplet had stood on frozen mountain peaks and burrowed into lightless caverns full of blind fish who talked in a language she couldn't understand no matter how hard she tried. But she'd never been to a city. She hadn't even seen Moss in a year, not since Moss's last visit to the colony. She hoped Moss would appreciate how much she'd grown.

Droplet and her mother approached their destination as seagulls. The thousand-year-old city sprawled beneath them like a living thing, a web of roots or the hidden tangle below a mushroom ring. While Droplet's mother attempted to find where they were going, Droplet took off in every direction. The green spires of temples to the Air Deity stretched higher than oak trees. Buildings of stone rearranged their upper stories as the hour chimed from dozens of bell towers. Statues of humans littered the city, along with a handful depicting raptors, griffins, and what had to be guardians, with their wings, their fanned feather tails, and the spells of fire and water that cascaded through their upraised arms. Droplet was about to try flying through one arcing jet when her mother cawed her back.

Summerbird had found the right street at last.

They landed on a straight street of flat, smooth cobblestones shaded by evenly spaced oaks. Behind the oak trees sat rows of brick-fronted homes joined together, like a small cliff face full of evenly spaced doors. The shrubbery in front of the homes had been trimmed into boxes. It was the most regimented thing Droplet had seen in her life. Was Moss being punished, living here?

Droplet and Summerbird hid in one unnaturally square shrub to change into cats—Droplet a gray kitten in the lanky, all-legs stage midway to adult, Summerbird as a hulking gray tom. The lines of the earth faded away, and blue washed over Droplet's vision, but each flutter of the air teased her newly sprouted whiskers with promises of critters to pounce on and sunbeams to lie in. Summerbird led the way to a door along the street and began scratching and yowling.

Soon, a hybrid answered the door.

Droplet had never seen a hybrid before, and her first, horrified thought was that a shapeshifter had gotten stuck. This one was half-eagle, covered in golden-brown feathers, standing tall as a human but with bird legs and a stubby beak. She wore a clip of the Sea Goddess in her crown feathers, a larger wave pendant around her neck, flowing gray pants, and a tight shirt of undyed cotton.

"More friends of Moss, I see," the eagle said with a sigh. "Come along, then."

Summerbird mewled in indignation at the rudeness, but followed.

The home they entered was paneled in dark wood, with rich green fabrics on nearly every surface—wall hangings, lampshades, carpet, cushions. Dozens of new smells jumbled over each other, but Droplet had no time to investigate them, not at the pace the half-eagle set. Following, the two shapeshifters trotted upstairs and down a narrow hallway to a sitting room.

"Visitors for Moss," the half-eagle said, walking over to a vacant seat. Inside the room, a bear, a half-dog, and a human sat in stuffed chairs before a cold fireplace. The human, a broad-shouldered one with a thick beard, started upon seeing the newcomers. The shock only lasted a moment, then was replaced by a joyous flood of recognition.

"Summerbird! My little Droplet!" The human disappeared, the clothes crumpling on suddenly empty air. A white-and-black cat struggled out of the clothing and bounded over to them.

Moss! Summerbird and Droplet exclaimed, bounding toward her in turn. The three cats nuzzled and butted their heads against each other. Moss smelled healthy and well-fed, with the scent of inside things layered over her fur—paper, polished wood, and soot.

Moss led them through the house to a room with a lavish human bed, four posts and curtains and everything. While her parents shifted into human forms, Droplet explored the bed, sniffing the blankets and pouncing on tassels. Moss offered up clothes for them to borrow, though it took a while for Moss to dig up a small robe that would do for Droplet. Droplet only had one human form, still, and she shifted into it, regretfully leaving the tassels behind. Clothed, the three of them returned to the sitting room.

Moss's friends hadn't left; when Droplet came back downstairs, they were pouring each other wine and passing around trays of cheeses, figs, grapes, and slices of vegetables she couldn't identify.

The bear drank from a wooden bowl while the others used crystal drinkware that caught the light of the room's lightstone chandelier. Droplet stared the most at the crystal glasses, though the whole room was surreal. Every object, from the walls to the clothes to the food, seemed at least three steps removed from the world of her colony.

After introductions, Summerbird told the story of the Cult of the Endless War's invasion. Droplet thought it was decidedly unfair for her mother to hog the storytelling joy for herself, considering her mother hadn't ever gone into the town. But she didn't want to disrespect her mother, especially in front of strangers. What would they think about Droplet?

Once the story was over, the bear, Nedrud, spoke to Droplet first. "You must be very brave, to have gone back to the town like that," he said.

Droplet felt like she'd grown three feet. "Thank you," she said.

Droplet wanted to know more about Moss's friends and about life here in Panithen, but Moss kept the conversation focused on her and Summerbird. Droplet decided to intervene. She was almost grown now, wasn't she? And she was brave, too; the bear had said so. She could join in the adult conversation.

"Do you all live here?" she asked as soon as the conversation paused.

"We do," said the half-eagle, Yelarcha. She had not said anything up to that point. Droplet thought she didn't like them much.

"Are you a colony, then?" she asked. She knew some shapeshifters settled down with other species. The adults of her colony liked to gossip about them, trading scandalous rumors, especially when they didn't realize she was listening.

"Droplet," her mother scolded her. But Droplet thought Moss was smiling behind her beard.

After a glance at Nedrud—so small Droplet almost didn't catch it—the red-and-white half-dog, Rangitam, said, "We're just friends working together." He raised his glass in a toast to the others.

"Hear, hear," said Moss.

Nedrud said, "Droplet, why doesn't Rangitam show you around the house? You must have so many more questions."

Droplet knew how to look for misdirection from adult shape-shifters; she had no experience reading the signs among hybrids. She spent a delightful couple hours exploring the house with Rangitam, asking him about the food in Panithen, what people did for fun, what kinds of people lived here—anything and everything that popped into her head. She didn't get suspicious until the third question Rangitam avoided about the group's life. Specifically, "What do you work on with Moss?"

"Oh, it's very boring. City stuff," Rangitam said.

One of two things must be true: either Rangitam was one of those condescending adults who thought children were no more than fledgling robins, or Rangitam was hiding something. She dearly hoped for the latter. She'd just left a whole colony of adults who had known her since infancy. She wanted these new adults to see her for who she was now.

Droplet had a bed of her own that night. She had no experience with beds; she burrowed under the covers, got too hot, twined the blankets around her into a nest, realized her limbs were trapped, became a mouse, then was awash in a sea of clothing and blankets with no sense of the way out. Turning into a fox, she found herself stuck in a sleeve.

Summerbird, still a human, came in to check on her and stifled a laugh. Droplet quashed her embarrassment; she had more important things to worry about. She squirmed out of the sleeve.

Mother, what are Moss and her friends hiding?

Summerbird sat down on the bed and began to scratch Droplet's head. Droplet nuzzled her. "That's their secret to tell, my darling.

I'm sure they will explain it to you when you're older."

Droplet stamped her paws, a much less satisfying motion on a soft mattress than on solid ground. **What's so secret that Moss can't tell me? Does Moss not trust me?**

"Oh my little one, of course Moss trusts you! But it's a dangerous secret to know. You'd be at risk, and neither of us want that for you." She kissed the top of Droplet's head. "You are a shapeshifter, my love. You are made to see hundreds of springtimes turn to summers. You will know the feel of clouds above mountain peaks and sand below deep seas. Not like the humans and raptors and their ilk. They will kill over the strangest things. A patch of ground not even big enough for a warren of rabbits. Love between two unexpected people. A pile of shiny rocks. Moss has gotten herself all mixed up with those people, and that means..." Summerbird swallowed hard. "When you're mixed up with these people, you become a target. You have to be older to choose that fate, my child."

Droplet thought of the bear at the table, looking at her almost as though she was a real adult. *"You must be very brave."*

She said, **I love you, Mother.**

"I love you too, my little Droplet."

Summerbird showed her how a human arranged bed sheets and pillows. After they exchanged goodnights, Droplet waited for ten minutes, until the hallway was all quiet, and became a chameleon.

As a shapeshifter, she adapted quickly to new senses and muscles. True, Droplet had bumped into a tree more than once from stunts like shifting straight from an owl's depth perception to a pigeon's wide, wide view. But even someone as young as Droplet could acclimatize to these changes in a matter of minutes.

A chameleon, though, was *weird*.

Droplet spent five whole minutes moving each eye independently before she left the bed. Next, she tried changing colors, watching her tail intently as she tried to match the wood of the floor. Then, she ran up the walls, the pads of her toes clinging to the wallpaper. She did her best to match the pale blue of this room. She managed to get to a greenish-bluish hue too saturated for the walls, decided it was close enough, and trundled into the hallway. She couldn't spend all night working on camouflage. She needed to hear what the adults were up to.

They'd moved to a basement kitchen with a wide table that they'd covered in diagrams and maps. Droplet entered the doorway as close to the roof as possible and crawled to a shadowed corner. The corner was cool, too cool for her lizard body's liking, but she ignored the chill and attempted to match the slate of this room's walls as she listened to the conversation. Moss's friends from earlier were all there, and her mother sprawled by the fire as a large dog. Everyone besides her mother stood around the table. Moss was nowhere to be seen.

"Any news on the getaway boat?" said Yelarcha.

"Not a thing. Doesn't Cromfogast have a pleasure boat? We could use that," said Nedrud.

"Oh sure, that won't be conspicuous at all," said Rangitam, his voice high and fast with nerves.

"Those boats are nothing but gilt and show. We tear off the trappings, it could be any old boat," Nedrud rumbled.

"Who's going to do that work? Moss will be at the pens," said Yelarcha, turning her eagle glare toward the bear.

Pens! A getaway boat! Destruction! Droplet trained both her chameleon eyes on the maps. She'd never been this excited. They were stealing something, obviously. But what? It couldn't be bad—her mother was there, and Moss was involved. She knew about maps, of course. For shapeshifters who wanted to earn some coin, mapmaking was one of the most prestigious jobs available. Shapeshifters could explore new lands and, at the same time, spread knowledge to those less-fortunate souls who couldn't fly. But Droplet had never met a mapmaker, let alone learned how to read maps.

One map involved a lot of blue. The other had large, connected, boxy shapes—a house?

Suddenly, whip-quick, Yelarcha rolled up the map. Summer-bird, on the floor, lumbered to her feet and stretched. The mission, whatever it was, was starting.

If Droplet wanted to follow them, she needed to get out of here. She tried to scurry. Instead, her legs moved like wading through honey, slow and unmanageable. Dread crept in—the cold wall had leached away the body heat her lizard body needed. In her excitement, she hadn't noticed her limbs stiffening. She could shift—shifting always generated warmth...but no, what if she fell off the wall? They'd be bound to notice her. She swiveled her eyes. At the ceiling, the basement had tiny windows cracked for ventilation, and the nearest was only a few body-lengths away. Slow step by slow step, she inched out, lizard footsteps inaudible under the rustle of paper and the murmur of final preparations.

She squeezed through the narrow window gap. The full chill of the evening air descended. Chameleons weren't built for this sort of weather. She shifted back into her cat form, fur sprouting from her skin like grass and fending off the cold from outside as her body resumed warming itself from within.

Powerful jaws grabbed the scruff of her neck and hoisted her into the air. Droplet squeaked. She was too old for this! She wasn't a kitten anymore! Sure, she wasn't all-the-way grown, but this was an indignity not to be borne.

She was carried down a narrow staircase and through a scuffed wooden door back into the basement. Her mother, Rangitam, and Yelarcha were still there to witness her humiliation. Droplet wished herself far, far away, but the wish did nothing. The jaws released her, and she plopped onto the floor; she looked up and behind, now that her neck was free. As a dog, Moss beamed down at her, tongue lolling.

Not tonight, but good spirit! she said. Reluctantly, Droplet turned to her mother.

Her mother's face drooped with sadness, dog eyes wide. Droplet had never felt so small. **I wanted to know, Mother**, Droplet said. Tail lashing, she scooted away from them both.

Moss's face had grown somber too. **If we tell you what's going on, you have to promise to stay inside**, Moss said. Droplet began to protest, but Moss continued, **This isn't forever, Droplet. You're getting older every day. But you must trust us that you're not old enough now.**

It's not something for shapeshifters, Summerbird said.

Moss barked.

It's not! Summerbird repeated.

You have your ideas about knowing the world, and I have mine, Moss said, a low growl accompanying her movements as she talked. The fur on her back began to rise.

Summerbird crouched until she was almost as low as Droplet, baring her teeth with an answering growl. **Some things aren't worth risking other people's lives**, Summerbird snapped.

Some things are, snarled Moss.

Not my Droplet's, said Summerbird.

Not until Droplet can make that choice herself, said Moss. She lowered her hackles. **I promise, Summerbird, that knowing is less of a risk than not at this point. You've raised a proper, inquisitive shapeshifter.**

The flattery seemed to work. Some of the tension left Summerbird's haunches. Moss closed the space between them and began to lick Summerbird's head.

Full of gratitude, Droplet nuzzled her mother. She tried not to show her excitement.

Moss had to leave on the secret mission, so Summerbird took Droplet back to the sitting room, where the bear lay on the ground looking over giant books of handwritten numbers. As the two shapeshifters entered, Nedrud lifted his enormous head. He didn't seem surprised to see either of them.

Nedrud is the mastermind. He likes you. He'll fill you in, Moss had explained before gallivanting off into the night.

"You can go to sleep if you'd like, Madam Summerbird," he said. Droplet's mother lay by the low fireplace full of the glowing coals of former logs, settling like a watchdog, all feet flat on the floor, head lifted and alert. Attempting to ignore her, Droplet turned into a griffin. She didn't care for her griffin form at this stage—it was midway through the molt from gray baby down to real, gold-brown feathers, and the new feathers itched. But she could talk to the bear in this form without bothering to put on clothes.

Nedrud folded the book with one massive paw.

"Have you met many hybrids?" he asked. Droplet shook her head. "Have you learned much about how human and raptor societies work?" She shook her head again. He nodded thoughtfully, tapping his claws against the carpet. "How about this. Do you know how humans and raptors treat other animals?"

"Oh yes," Droplet said, bobbing her fuzzy head.

"Then that's where we'll start." He looked at the carpet for several moments—Droplet assumed he was gathering his thoughts—and began. "How we got this way doesn't matter; here's what you need to know. In cities...in countries...raptors and humans are the ones with all the power. And some of them like us fine. But most of them think we're more like animals—and you know how they treat animals. Now some of us hybrids go before courts and nobles and counselors to try and sway the law of the land so we will have some power from time to time. This is important work, taken on by people with more strength and fortitude than me." He paused again to shift his massive bulk. "My friends and I, Moss among them, take a more direct approach."

He drummed his claws once more, with intent. The wicked curves sunk deep into the fabric and stabbed the wood beneath.

Chapter Eight

Droplet disrobed in their inn room, tucking her clothes into their traveling packs alongside the far-speak charms. She and Azera at least agreed on the need to be prepared for a quick getaway.

"Can you turn into one of the barn cats?" Azera said.

Droplet grimaced. *She doesn't mean to be insulting. She doesn't know. You don't* want *her to know shapeshifter secrets.* Aloud, Droplet said, "I have a gray cat form. One of the cats out there was gray. It will be close enough."

"There's a lot of variety in 'gray cat,' " Azera said.

Droplet waved a hand. "Humans and raptors won't notice. Especially with a cat they've probably seen once. If they spot that I'm different, they'll just think the inn has more cats."

"Fair. Okay." Azera hefted both traveling packs, up and down and up again, and her foot drummed on the floor. She looked more nervous than Droplet felt, which was a feat. "Good luck."

Droplet nodded and shifted.

After more than a day as a human, the transformation to cat felt luxurious. Her muscles and bones flowed like liquid metal. Even her still-healing chest wound barely bothered her, pain negligible compared to the relief of having new senses, mobility, and energy. At a tenth of her human size, she felt ten times more powerful.

Her tail lashed without her say-so as she sniffed the air and listened. Even though the crowd had shrunk, the chatter from the common room was jumbled and lively. The occasional voice leapt out from the mass, enough for her to tell that the blood mages still haunted that room.

Azera opened the door for her, and she sauntered into the hallway.

Acting like a real cat, at least when trying to convince non-felines that she was a cat, followed the same principles as acting like a real wealthy person. All Droplet had to do was assume she was the smartest person in the room.

True, the act was harder with a room full of blood mages. But with a cat's coiled energy thrumming under her skin, with claws and teeth ready to bare, Droplet thought she could still give a good show.

As if I couldn't do this alone, she thought, and let the resentment strengthen her steps.

The jumbled threads of smells in the inn resolved into a vibrant tapestry clear to her cat nose. Three other cats moved through this room regularly. Lucky for her in some ways—she didn't need any of the inn workers chasing her out. But if any of the cats came to investigate this stranger, she'd have some explaining to do.

Her inborn cat form, satisfyingly, had grown into a barrel of a queen. She walked into the common room like she owned it. She smelled mice in a distant corner and sauntered that way, weaving around the tables. For show, she sniffed at the occasional morsel of fallen food. The mice scrabbled into their bolt holes well before she reached the wall. Good. She didn't want to torment an innocent mouse to keep up a cat illusion.

A table next to the blood mages had opened up. Droplet hopped onto the bench and proceeded to wash herself. The dust of a day's travel that had been on her human skin still rested on her fur, and the scrape of her tongue soothed her nerves from "Imminent death ahead!" to merely "Danger! Danger!"

The blood mages chattered about inconsequential nothings. Like Solvim, they had been traveling, and they shared tales from their respective journeys to different cities, as far south as Owl's

Point and as far west as the Pinewilds. The magpie-colored raptor had come to meet them from Sacarus, but nobody was kind enough to specify from *where* in Sacarus. A human with a long braid spotted Droplet and leaned back from the table, stretching out a hand. "Here kitty! Here kitty!"

Before Droplet could think, she crouched, ears flat, tail whipping like a flag in a high wind. The raptor who'd drank so quickly laughed uproariously at his traveling companion and smacked her on the shoulder.

"No wonder it's skittish, if you keep doing that," said the braided human with a sniff. She tried again. "Come on! Come on!"

Droplet steeled her nerves and leaned forward, sniffing deeply. *Haughty. Aloof. Superior*, she reminded herself. She smelled old blood on the human, but old blood only, nothing fresh enough for active magic. Relieved, she nonetheless turned up her nose and returned to washing herself, attempting to radiate indifference as she licked her paw. The braided human's companions pulled her back to the table.

When the blood mages got onto the topic of leverball, and when it became clear that none of the many leverball teams they supported were from Sacarus, Droplet took a stroll around the room. She ventured through an open back door, even, to walk to the stables. But most of the garzis were asleep, and the stable housed dozens—finding the blood mages' mounts could take hours. Not a promising lead.

A clanging noise rang out from the inn. Droplet raced back, tail fluffed. Had the blood mages acted? No...no, just the inn proprietor, a fluffy, chestnut-feathered raptor, banging a pot to tell his patrons to clear out for the night. Slowly, with varying levels of disgruntlement, the remaining tables dispersed. Droplet draped herself over a stack of crates outside the kitchen to watch where the blood mages went. But they didn't move. One of them called over the proprietor, and after a short conversation, the proprietor let them be, saying, "Sleep on the tables for all I care, as long as you keep the noise down."

Keeping out of the proprietor's line of sight—surely he would recognize his own cats—Droplet jumped from the crates and began to saunter amidst the tables again.

With the rest of the crowd gone, the blood mages began really talking.

"So, Solvim," the black-and-white raptor said, examining her uncapped claws.

"Yes, Isna," said Solvim.

"Remind me, please, why we memorize the names of those who join our sacred quest," said Isna through a smile that showed off her fangs.

"To honor their sacrifice and keep their memory alive, even if they may choose to give the memory of their name to the guardians," Solvim recited.

"Is it so we can blurt out their name to suspicious travelers?" Isna asked sweetly.

"No, Isna," said Solvim.

The braided mage and a couple others laughed at him.

"You think they suspected us?" said the heavy drinker.

Isna covered her eyes with one feathery hand.

"Obviously," said a human man with a luxurious beard halfway through the process of going white.

"Who are these two, anyway?" said a gray raptor with white-speckled feathers.

Solvim summarized everything he remembered about "Dalere" and Azera. Droplet leapt to the bench near the braided human again, who turned away from the tense conversation to try and coax Droplet-the-cat into friendliness once more.

"Maybe Harra has said something," said the bearded man. "Someone should be watching the far-speak chamber, right?"

"If they value their positions, yes," Isna said coolly. From a deep blue traveling bag, she pulled out a far-speak disc—a nice one, the size of her hand, positioned within a sphere of thinly braided metal for safety. She spoke the words of command.

A perky voice echoed from the sphere, nearly as clear as if the speaker was in the room themselves. "Dedicate Merrite, at your service."

"Merrite, it's Isna. What can you tell me about Harra Virri-daughter?"

Droplet nearly purred in satisfaction. Now they were getting somewhere. She once again made a show of sniffing the braided human's hand, then turning away imperiously.

"Harra...Harra...she got here this morning. Is something wrong?" said Merrite.

"Two humans are on their way to Sacarus to look for her. They've got a fake story about why she's gone, but they might know we have her."

"Oh, right! Harra was the one from the Ninuthen docks, remember? She fought back, and she had a shapeshifter with her."

Silence.

As one, the table of blood mages turned to look at Droplet.

"Zamit, would you be so kind as to grab that cat?" Isna said, her voice like honeyed poison.

The braided human reached out her hand once more.

Droplet bolted, ears flat, tail puffed, heart racing. Behind her, the blood mages erupted into shouts, leapt to their feet, and gave chase.

Chapter Nine

Droplet easily outpaced the mages, zipping under the tables that tripped up the larger creatures. The room passed in a blur. The door to the bedroom flew open as Droplet approached; Azera stepped back to let Droplet bolt in, then whirled to grab their packs.

"Blood and bones," Azera swore as the racket of mages approached. "Get out, get out!" She strode to the window and flung it open.

No time to plan; no time to talk. The mages—Solvim at the head of the pack—were steps from the door. Droplet smelled fresh blood as Solvim charged in and raised his hands.

For the second time in as many days, Droplet couldn't think of what to do. Terror spun her mind into useless circles. Blood mages had trapped her before, even when she had bone charms. She could distract them from Azera while Azera got out the window, but for how long? Could she take even one of them down?

A couple agonizing moments of panic passed before Droplet—and Solvim—realized that whatever he was trying to do, it wasn't working. He looked down at his hands and shook them as if they were the problem.

Maybe he's a weaker mage, Droplet thought. *Maybe Azera has a lot of dragon bones on her.* Azera hadn't left the room, had she? Droplet hadn't heard her climb out the window.

Droplet turned.

Azera's eyes glittered in the darkness, reflecting an icy blue light that Droplet couldn't see. She brought her hands together.

Without a sound, the room filled with ghosts.

Solvim and the mages on his heels screamed. The ghosts, four, all human, drifted toward the mages, raising their wrinkled, translucent hands and moaning like wind through trees.

"We only wanted to talk," Solvim said, his words strangled.

"Good. Talk," Azera said. "Where's Harra?" The ethereal moans subsided, but the ghosts spread out to flank the two blood mages.

"She's perfectly safe, I promise," he said. "You have us all wrong. It's an honor to be chosen."

One of the ghosts blocked the door. Droplet shifted from foot to foot. Now that the initial shock had worn off, she assessed the situation with as much detachment as she could muster. Ghosts couldn't *do* anything to the living, as far as she knew. Sure, they'd knock out any magic in the room—maybe even in several rooms— but if Solvim and his friends had even one non-magic weapon on them, Azera was history.

Solvim nattered on. "She's not going to do anything except of her own free will. You'll see. We only ask for a few memories, nothing more. We're giving her a chance to be part of something grand."

"Considering you kidnapped my friend, stuck her in a crate, and shipped her off to gods-know-where, I don't think much of your grandeur. Tell me where she is," Azera said.

"Or what?" said the bearded human.

That was Droplet's cue. She became a Nortakian tundra wolf, the largest canid form she had, with jaws that could bite through a human arm.

The bearded human produced a long, hollow metal cylinder from under his cloak; Droplet stared at it without recognition for a moment before identifying it as that Ganlian magekiller called a *gun*.

Azera scrambled out the window, both packs bouncing on her back. Droplet followed, claws catching and slipping on the sheets of the bed as she leapt after. The shutters banged wide as she heaved her shoulders through, scraping them against the sides of the window frame.

Out in the courtyard, Isna and the braided mage waited.

Azera raised her hands. More ghosts appeared as she looked left and right, scanning for a way out. Terror poured off Azera, and fresh blood oozed from the two mages, the smells overpowering everything else in the stable yard.

Droplet paused. Azera was a necromancer. Necromancers tore the dead from their rightful rest and enslaved them. They sabotaged magic wherever they went. They murdered people to add them to armies of undead.

That's what people said, anyway.

Droplet knew what people said about necromancers, but she also knew what humans said about shapeshifters.

She became a garzi, and the smells faded to almost nothing. She galloped the short distance to Azera, folded her front legs beneath her, and spread her stumpy vestigial wings, squawking. Azera looked down at her, eyes wild and still glittering blue. Droplet squawked again. The blood mages flanking them weren't going to wait around.

"I've never ridden without a saddle before!" Azera said. Droplet gave her best *Are you serious?* look. A shot burst from inside the room; the bullet hit the ground near Azera's feet. "Now is a great time to try!"

Azera swung onto Droplet's back, throwing her legs behind the wing joints and wrapping her muscular arms tight around Droplet's neck. Droplet bounded to her feet and forward, Azera yelping with the jolt.

Another shot rang out behind her. She sprinted for the edge of the courtyard while Isna and the braided mage stood powerless against the void of magic Azera had created. She galloped through the stables, through the front courtyard, and onto the road, her powerful claws kicking up gravel. Legs knocking against Droplet's feathery sides, arms nearly strangling her, Azera clung on for dear life.

Together, they fled north.

Only when Droplet couldn't run any more, heaving lungs and throbbing legs united in protest, did she stop running. She slowed to catch her breath, just for a moment, except when she tried to pick up speed again, she nearly fell over.

"Droplet, stop," Azera said. "They're gone. We're okay."

She cawed in protest. But blood mages were, of course, limited by the amount of blood they could safely lose in one sitting. They probably wouldn't be able to chase them up the road magically. If they all had garzis... Well, Droplet was in no shape to keep running. She turned from the road into the pines surrounding it. Azera slipped from her back, landed sprawled on the ground, and leapt to her feet as Droplet looked back at her. "I'm fine. Fine."

Once Droplet made it behind the trees, she shifted into a human, the Dalere form, and sprawled face down in the pine needles, panting. The cool air felt fantastic on her skin, and soon she was sweating profusely. For all their flaws in form, humans certainly had thermoregulation worked out.

"Thank you," Azera said, breaking through Droplet's exhaustion.

"For what?" Droplet said.

"For getting me out of there. I'm very grateful. You didn't have to do that."

Droplet pushed herself partially off the ground and twisted her neck so she could see Azera. The human sat curled in on herself, arms clutching legs. Droplet couldn't see her face in the darkness. "What kind of person would I be if I didn't?" she asked.

Azera sobbed, sinking to the ground.

Droplet froze. It had been years since she'd needed to comfort a human. She sat up, remembered that humans generally opposed nudity except in special circumstances, saw that both bags were supporting Azera's back, and decided to stay naked for now.

"It's going to be okay," Droplet ventured. This wasn't necessarily true, given that the blood cultists now knew who they were, but it at least entered the realm of reassurance. "We can outrun them, and you shut down their magic—handy—so I'd say we're in pretty good shape."

Azera continued sobbing. "And you're okay with this? Just like that?"

Droplet was about to say something like, "No, the blood mages could have killed me, don't you recognize when someone's putting on a brave face?" But then the pieces fell together, and Droplet realized what Azera meant by "this."

"Your fiancée didn't take well to finding out you were a necromancer, did she," Droplet said quietly.

Azera took a few deep breaths and wiped her face on her sleeve. "My parents told me not to tell her," she said, voice hoarse. "So I didn't. Not for ages. They said she'd leave me if she knew, and they couldn't risk that. She was rich. She had connections. We would have taken a bigger step up in the world than my family had ever dreamed of. We've been carpenters for generations. But necromancy was my secret to tell. None of my parents are necromancers, none of my siblings, none of my living grandparents. Just me. And I wanted her to..." Azera broke off to gulp another few breaths.

"I wanted her to love me anyway. I really thought she would. But she said she couldn't trust me because I'd kept something like that from her for so long. Ironic, right? I haven't told my parents why she cut me off. They're terrified of what'll happen if it gets out that we have necromancy in our blood. It would ruin my brothers' prospects of getting married." Azera scuffed her foot into the dirt. "But I was too selfish to think about that. Too stupid. Too hopeful." She had scratched a deep furrow already with the force of her foot. "So that's my story. That's why I was out with Harra, the only living person who doesn't hate what I am. That's why I couldn't turn to anyone else."

Silence reigned.

Droplet did her best to control her voice. Azera was very fragile right now and would probably break at any loud noises. "Among shapeshifters, there is no crime so foul as abandoning your child," Droplet growled.

Azera looked up from her legs, although who knew if she could see anything in this light. "Really?" she said.

"Your parents are *your parents*. They should be the ones who support you without question. They have failed you."

After a long pause, Azera's next words came out choked. "Thank you."

Droplet reached over and laid her hand on Azera's shoulder. Azera didn't say anything, so Droplet patted her shoulder a few times. She wished she'd spent more time learning about how Makidan humans typically comforted each other. She had a sneaking suspicion awkward shoulder pats didn't cut it.

"So...you're okay with necromancy?" Azera asked again.

"It's no more disturbing than human death and souls in general," Droplet said.

"Human souls are disturbing?"

"Yes. You go on existing as only yourself after you die, separate forever, like...like a rock, or a cactus, or something. Much more depressing than rejoining the star-walker and becoming a part of shapeshifters yet to be born."

In the pause that followed, Droplet tensed.

"I'm making a list, you know. A very long list. Of all the questions I have for you when this is over." Droplet's eyes had begun to adjust to the darkness, enough to see Azera turn and smile at her. "My grandmother will be here soon," Azera said. "You should probably put clothes on."

"Yes. Yes, I should," Droplet said. Azera handed over the bag.

"Your grandmother is..."

"Dead, yes."

Droplet had barely tugged on a shirt when Azera's eyes glittered blue again, sparks in the darkness, and a ghost popped into view. An old woman with Azera's wide eyes, she was dressed in a wrapped skirt and a top with sleeves that drooped nearly to the ground. Droplet sat up straighter and tried to brush pine needles off her pants.

"Hello there!" said Azera's grandmother. Her deep voice was clearer than Droplet would have expected from the dead, with only a faint resonance, as if she stood in a well the living couldn't see. "Droplet! So nice to finally meet you face-to-face."

"It's an honor to meet you," Droplet said, bowing at the waist.

"Please, no need for that," Azera's grandmother said with a laugh. "I'm just happy to meet someone helping my grandbaby out."

"It is always an honor to meet a mother of mothers," said Droplet. "Shapeshifters know this."

"Shapeshifters are smart people. We should be taking notes," Azera's grandmother said.

"So...the blood mages," Azera prompted. In the faint light cast by the ghost, Droplet could see a hint of a smile on the living woman's face.

"They aren't chasing you, but I think they've sent word ahead to people in Sacarus," said the ghost.

"Forgive me my ignorance, but have you been with us the whole time?" Droplet asked.

"Oh yes. I watched you on the docks, too. What an incredible performance!"

"Ohhh, so Harra was talking to *you*, not me," Droplet said.

"Harra's a smart young woman; I'm sure the information was meant to help both of us," Azera's grandmother said diplomatically. "Once the mages took her, I followed you to your house, then returned to my granddaughter. I can always find her."

"Is that a necromancer thing or a ghost thing?" Droplet asked.

"A ghost thing," Azera said.

"We ghosts can always find our way back to the people who are part of our unresolved business in the living world," her grandmother said, as light and pleasant as a conversation over desserts. Azera looked down, and Droplet didn't push further. "I've followed you since you left the manor. I would love to be of more help, but it's hard for me to get close to the blood mages on the plane of the dead. Such strong magic distorts our plane, you see. Unsettling."

"You were plenty of help back there," Azera protested. "You brought the other ghosts in."

"You don't know those ghosts?" Droplet asked.

"No, no, I met them this evening. Such kind people! I shall have to make a trip back there when everything has settled down. We got to talking about our grandchildren, our hobbies...you know how it is."

Droplet did not.

"Grandma spent most of the evening making friends, and she asked them to be ready in case we needed them. A lot of them agreed, as you saw," said Azera.

So there had been another option all along. Droplet scuffed her foot along the ground. "The spying backfired," she said, though she couldn't quite bring herself to say Azera was right. After all, Droplet had been working with all the information she had. "It's good you had a back-up plan."

"I'm glad you're a sensible young woman. This whole rescue mission will be much easier now that my Azera can openly use necromancy with you," said Azera's grandmother.

Azera said nothing. Droplet recognized the mixture of love and embarrassment of a fellow adult being parented. And thinking of parents...

"We need to tell Moss we've been discovered," Droplet said.

"I don't know if we can," Azera said apologetically. "I summoned a *lot* of ghosts. It probably wiped clean any spells in the room."

She was right. When Droplet tried the far-speak discs, they sat inert, ordinary and useless metal once more.

I'm the leader, now, Droplet thought with a pang of fear. No Moss to guide her. Nobody to turn to. At least until they got to Sacarus—Rangitam would be waiting for them there. Rangitam knew what he was doing, and he was in touch with Moss. All they had to do was make it into Sacarus. A full day's journey with blood mages in pursuit.

With an immense force of will, Droplet refrained from immediately sprinting down the road.

As riding the mail coach was no longer an option, the only sensible way forward was walking.

Azera took the first shift. Droplet, still exhausted from the run, became a green-speckled warbler, a perching bird that could sleep on the straps of their travel bags without falling off. As Azera set out north on the road, Droplet fell asleep.

They were nearly a day of normal travel out from Sacarus. But by taking shifts, they aimed to reach Sacarus well before the next sundown.

Droplet woke up to Azera saying her name. Groggy, she flittered to the ground and became a garzi, wobbling as her back legs grew underneath her and her warbler wings migrated forward into legs. Why the wings became legs, Droplet had no idea, as this transition always meant sprouting extra wings on her back. Why couldn't the wings stay wings, and why didn't she grow new legs instead? It was the same every time transitioning between four limbs and six...garzis, griffins, wyverns...

Azera tapped her shoulder, and she jumped, shaking herself out of her half-asleep wondering. Azera clambered on, wincing, and they were off again.

Garzis were not built for the night. Anything could be moving in the pines. Walking in the middle of the road, Droplet tried to keep herself awake using fear alone. As Azera nodded off the first time, she and the bags started sliding, and Droplet hurriedly arranged her stubby wings to support the wobbly load.

Sleep was hard to come by for both of them. A rocking shoulder, a shifting bag, a feathery back...none were what Droplet would call comfy, even without the threat of deranged blood mages and their worry for captured Harra.

Inevitably, Azera and Droplet started talking.

"You know a lot about me at this point, but I don't know much about you," Azera said. She was doing a shift walking, and Droplet sat on her shoulder as a dull-gray parrot.

"An accurate observation," Droplet said.

Azera snorted. "Do you feel like changing that?" Droplet thought about this. And thought. And thought. "Okay, okay. Basic stuff. Which god do you actually follow?"

"Sea Goddess," Droplet said. That was truly a surface-level question here in Makido. You had to know a person's patron deity to even address them properly. She had to catch herself on travels through Nortak and Ganlia, where religion was a fraught topic.

"Why?"

"Now that is not the basic stuff," Droplet said. Not taboo, but personal.

"Yeah, but I figured, you saw me crying on the ground, and you know my worst secret. I'd like to at least learn a bit about you, mystery shapeshifter."

Droplet wanted to draw her shell in tighter, but relented. Azera didn't have the luxury of a shell anymore. Opening up a crack would be only fair. "Most shapeshifters follow the Sea Goddess. Almost all of them."

"Really? No matter how they're born?"

"Really. We're sworn to the Sea Goddess at birth, and very few change away. Honestly, it's weird that more Makidans don't choose her. She's the most deadly of the four."

"That's...one way of picking a god," Azera said.

"What other reason would there be?" Droplet said. "For shapeshifters...we can burrow, we've mapped cave systems humans could never find, we've soared as high as dragons, and we can navigate a river in hundreds of different bodies. The sea *keeps going down*. Nobody has ever found the deepest ocean floor, not even shapeshifters. We don't know where it ends. But we've seen things with too many tentacles and too few eyes and glowing orbs on their heads. A dead sea serpent as long as an oak tree is tall washed ashore a few years ago, when I was up in Nortak. And you know what it died of? Bites. And..." Droplet stopped herself. Her feathers were fluffing up, as if she was under attack and needed to frighten off a predator. Her bird heartbeat, usually a patter like falling rain, had become a frantic race.

"And?" Azera prompted.

"And shapeshifters keep going down there, because we have to find out what's there. A lot don't come back." Droplet shifted from scaly foot to scaly foot.

"I'm sorry," Azera said. She fell silent and didn't ask why they had to keep going down there, which was good, because Droplet wouldn't have answered. Already Droplet worried she'd shared too much. Azera would be gone from her life in a few days, after all. No reason to give shapeshifter secrets away to a human when she didn't know what the human would do with them later.

When Droplet had begun to unfluff her feathers, Azera commented, "It sounds harsh, not having much of a say in what deity you worship."

"It sounds worse to not have any say in your species, but somehow humans manage," Droplet said.

"Point taken. But doesn't it get confusing, changing all the time? Thumbs one minute, claws the next? Two legs, then four?"

"Only sometimes. Like when we're really tired, and sore, and chased by blood mages."

"Ah. Is there a better shape for times like this?" Azera said.

Was...was that concern in her voice? How unnecessary. But sweet. But unnecessary. "I like birds. Most of us have favorite shapes—shapes that feel comfortable, or shapes that show who we are."

Azera brightened. "Oh? And what are you like?"

"A goose," Droplet said with some pride. She was surprised when Azera cracked up. "What's so funny about that?" she demanded.

"The noble vigilante, defender of the weak...the mighty goose!"

"Geese are very strong," Droplet protested.

"I'm sorry, I'm just picturing it...a voice cries out for help in the darkness of Ninuthen, and in the mouth of the alleyway, a savior appears—a goose!"

"You clearly have never met a goose. You'd be properly impressed if you had."

"Its mighty honk strikes fear into the bones of evildoers!"

"You're enjoying this too much."

"Cower before its webbed feet of justice—"

Droplet did the only thing she could at this point: become a goose. Azera yelped, toppling over from the sudden weight on her shoulder as Droplet thwacked her with three-foot wings. Buffeted by feathers, she lay giggling in the dust of the road. Droplet hissed and stretched head and wingtips to their farthest length, a pose that would have struck fear into any lake-dwelling animal.

Azera lifted her head, took in the majestic sight, and whispered, "Honk."

Droplet's snaky neck drooped as the human collapsed into laughter again.

Chapter Ten

As Droplet grew from child to young adult, she spent more time with Moss and the merry band in Panithen. The band grew slowly, as did she. Most of the new arrivals were hybrids, from a talking garzi through a human covered in blue feathers. Almost every day, Droplet felt the shapeshifter thrill of seeing something new, something entirely hers that no other shapeshifter had seen, and she took pride in how much she'd be able to share with the Enduring Archive on her very first journey, when she would receive her true name. Though Summerbird fussed and fretted, she admitted that her daughter was becoming, as Moss said, "a proper, inquisitive shapeshifter."

Droplet's visits to Moss grew longer, until the trips to her colony were the visits. The four-poster bed in the Panithen house was hers now, though she shared it with a shapeshifter friend from her home colony. They were both still Droplets. At home, they'd been "Summerbird's Droplet" and "Granite's Droplet"; here, the other members of the organization avoided confusion by giving them each a host of nicknames. Ten years on, and Droplet was "Sport," while the younger Droplet was "Moonshine."

Ten years on, and "Sport" still hadn't been on a proper vigilante mission.

Sure, by shapeshifter reckoning, she wasn't an adult yet. But in years, she was older than some of the non-shifter recruits. She argued about this often with Moss, as her parent, and Nedrud, as leader of the group. But still, she was stuck on backup work. An apprentice, not a real partner. She bought food for the household and learned to cook, even to cook meat (she didn't tell her mother). She watched over the children of full members.

Often, she read records.

The organization had many ways of taking down corrupt people who abused hybrids. Blackmail was a favorite. When Droplet did manage to break free of domestic life, she was stuck poring over the books in counting houses, port authorities, and occasionally on personal estates.

Moss claimed this was proper vigilante work, full of infiltration and intrigue.

Droplet said proper vigilante work involved stalking the night, battling wicked guards while rescued hybrids fled into the night, and confronting evildoers on rooftops.

Moss said she and Moonshine read too many serials.

On one particular day, Droplet, as a raptor, sat in the study of a human nobleman, Lord Lengham, attempting to decipher the handwriting of whoever kept the household records. The nobleman had definitely been cheating laborers at his orchards out of money. But Nedrud and Moss were sure he was also smuggling mage-killing weapons—bone blades from Nortak and some new-fangled creations called "guns" from Ganlia. In Panithen, all the nobles were mages. If they thought one of their own was conspiring against them, they'd turn on them quicker and more effectively than sharks on a bleeding tuna. The organization could get the laborers their fair pay in all the confusion.

All Nedrud's group had to do was find some evidence.

Even though she'd kept her raptor shape the whole way, Droplet had snuck into the study without being seen. Lord Lengham and his household were out at some all-day society gala. Most of the household staff had the day off. The study itself was cool and comfortable, with plush chairs, an expansive desk, and towering shelves and cabinets lining three of the walls: a façade of order. Lengham's files mocked organization, handwriting, and consistency, requiring all Droplet's attention to parse.

So by the time she noticed the creak of footsteps outside the door, she had no time even to shift.

A human entered—blond, muscled, and scowling, wearing shapeless servants' robes of white and green. The scowl turned to shock at the sight of Droplet.

"Who are you?" he asked.

"Who are *you*?" Droplet snapped. She did not expect this tactic to work, but the man hesitated.

He seemed young. But he rallied, and the scowl reappeared. "The staff didn't mention that anyone was already here," he said.

"And they didn't mention you'd be coming. Do you have an appointment?" Droplet said, imitating Yelarcha at her haughtiest.

Objectively, this was a terrible bluff. If this man had any legitimate reason for being here, her act would fall apart in five seconds. Instead, he hesitated more, not meeting her eyes. "I should call the staff on you," he said.

"But you're not," Droplet said.

They held their positions. A clock on the flowery wall ticked off the seconds. The human did seem young, probably somewhere around Droplet's own twenty years. He smelled like livestock.

"I won't say anything if you don't," Droplet said.

The human nodded firmly and strode to the records. "What are you looking for?" he asked.

"Evidence of smuggling. You?"

"Lord Lengham broke his contract with my parents," the young man said. His voice choked up. He must be more nervous than he was showing. "They've been stuck working his orchard for my whole life and have more debt than when they started. I want proof that they can take to him."

"Right, he's obviously doing that, but evidence won't help," said Droplet.

"What?!"

"How do you think he's gotten away with it for so long? The rest of the nobles are just as bad. They don't care," she said as if explaining addition to a cub. Humans could be slow with this sort of thing, Moss and Nedrud had told her.

The human crossed his arms and looked coldly at her. "I'm not going to let my parents spend the rest of their lives rotting away under him."

Droplet approved of his loyalty. Perhaps this human could learn. She didn't talk to humans much, not anymore. The rare times she returned to the mountain colony, she spent time among shapeshifters, not the mountain villagers she'd once known.

"Who said anything about letting your parents rot? There's a better way," she said.

The man considered this. He looked at the mess of papers she'd spread across the desk of the study. "Who *are* you?"

"Not important," she said. "Can you read?"

"Yes."

"What do you know about guns?"

When Droplet returned home, the headquarter residents were locked in an intense battle of the card game chimney, a favorite in the house—a favorite with many other conspirators, too, but most of them kept separate homes. Nedrud and Yelarcha always played as a team, as Yelarcha, unlike Nedrud, had opposable thumbs. Moss, Rangitam, and Moonshine made up the rest of the players. At the table, Moss and Moonshine wore human form; humans had the best fingers for card-playing.

"You want in?" said Moss.

"Always," said Droplet. She sat between Moss and Moonshine as play continued.

"What's the news?" Nedrud said.

"We've got him," Droplet said smugly. She produced a beat-up records book from her inner robe pocket. "Only one piece of evidence so far, but he's been stockpiling guns for nearly as long as they've existed. Not sure yet who he's selling to."

Cheers and congratulations all around. Moss and Moonshine patted her on the back, the latter much more forcefully.

Into the general jubilation, Droplet said, "Also, there was a human in the records room with me." Perhaps, she thought, the good mood would help soften the news or make the team more receptive.

Tension spiked, smiles vanished, and Yelarcha's feathers all puffed out. If this was receptive, she'd hate to see the non-receptive reaction.

Droplet shared the story: a young human, looking to save his parents but with no way forward. He'd helped her search, and though he was slower than she was, two sets of eyes sped the hunt.

"What did you tell him?" Nedrud said, calmly.

"That I was part of a group of people working to take down the nobleman. Nothing else," said Droplet.

"Still too much information if he talks," muttered Moonshine.

"You could have done better?" Droplet muttered back.

Moss held up a hand to stop them. "Allies are always useful."

"If you can trust them," said Yelarcha.

"We don't have to trust this human with everything to use him," Nedrud said. He nudged Yelarcha with his massive paw. "Go on, play. It's our turn. We'll sort out the details later. Droplet, you've done well under pressure."

Not even her crushing defeats over ten rounds of chimney could dampen the pride Droplet felt.

Droplet returned to Lord Lengham's study the next day. Though the family had returned from their social outing, and though the number of servants in the house had tripled, Droplet still managed to sneak in undetected thanks to some quick shifting. It helped that she'd had the foresight to carry a separate pouch for her clothes.

The young human wasn't so lucky.

"I panicked and told them I was an inspector so they led me here, but we have to be quick."

"Why would you tell them you were an inspector?" Droplet said, flinging up her feathery raptor arms in frustration. "We *know* he's doing shady business. He'll be here in minutes once he hears there's an inspector in the house."

"What if he recognizes me?" the human moaned. He sank to the ground, putting his head in his hands. "He'll go after my family, he'll retaliate, he did that to the Brush family, I still don't know where they—"

"Listen. Listen, I need to find as much information as I can before they get here. You get out."

"How? The house is packed! Why do you think I got caught in the first place? How'd *you* get in?"

"Magic," Droplet said tersely.

"Wish I was rich enough for that," the human grumbled.

"I'm a *shapeshifter*, you ass, not all magic makes you rich," she snapped. She immediately regretted it.

His eyes went wide. "You're a shapeshifter? We're saved!"

"Flattering, but I'm sorry, what?"

"You turn into me. I hide, then when they show up, you turn into something else and escape! I'll wait until they leave and bring you the records later."

She said, "That's a terrible idea. No."

He said, "Can you think of a better plan? *Right now?*"

"I can't just *turn into you*," Droplet said.

"You can't?"

"We're *honoring people* when we take on new forms! It's part of our sacred duty! We can't go picking up new shapes on a whim," she said. She wanted to run. This was against everything the colony taught. Her colony took on barely a shape per moon, and they'd only taken on two human forms in Droplet's whole lifetime.

"Oh," he said. He stood up slowly and headed over to the books. "I'll read what I can, then. Can...can you get my parents out after this? He'll go after them when he sees it's me here." He swallowed back a sob.

If he'd tried to argue, or stall, or do anything else, Droplet would have said yes.

But she looked at the tears in his eyes and said, "Get over here. You cannot tell *anyone* about this, *ever*," she said.

He actually gasped. "Thank you, thank you, thank you," he babbled. "How does it work? Do you need to touch me, or—"

"I need to bite you."

He paused halfway to her. "You need to...bite me."

"I need to *eat* some of you, yes. It doesn't have to be a lot," Droplet said impatiently.

"I guess it could be worse," the man said. He finished walking up to her, rolled up his sleeve to his shoulder, and looked away.

Raptor teeth were sharp. Droplet would have preferred a smaller form for this, but they had so little time to spare. She tried to bite with just a corner of her mouth, keeping away from the major vessels.

The human grunted but didn't scream.

Gods, Droplet didn't even know his *name*. She *hated* this. At least human flesh didn't taste terrible. She swallowed and felt the prickly shiver of a new shape mingling with her blood.

"What's your name?" she asked.

"Forsyth Carrower."

She'd seen some liquor in the study shelves and grabbed a bottle. The human poured some over the bite mark while Droplet

tore part of her robe to wrap over the wound. They established a
rendezvous point as they worked. It was quick and efficient. The
human clearly had experience caring for wounds. But even with
their speed, by the time Droplet tied off the makeshift bandage,
they heard footsteps pounding up the stairs.

"Hurry," she whispered, because it felt better than saying nothing at all. He squeezed into one of the cabinets along the wall as
Droplet shifted.

Her tail sucked back into her body while her leg bones shrank
and grew. Her talons withdrew to form stubby human toes, and
she stood barefoot on the floor. In a hasty attempt to complete the
illusion, she wrapped the raptor-shaped robe tighter around herself. Thank goodness the colors were the same as Forsyth's robe.
The impersonation wouldn't hold up for long, but it didn't have to.

And once Droplet was done, nobody would be focusing on little
details like the size of clothes.

Lord Lengham himself burst through the door, vibrating with
indignation, burgundy clothes disheveled from his rush. House
servants, humans and raptors, flocked behind him like agitated
ducklings. He drew himself to his full height, more than a head
shorter than Forsyth's form. Droplet wondered whether Forsyth
realized how puny the lord was.

"What is the meaning of this?" he bellowed. He took in Droplet,
and his scowl turned to a gloating grin with the speed of an arrow.
"Young Forsyth, isn't it?"

"No," said Droplet.

She became a goose.

If Lord Lengham had reacted quicker, that might have saved
him. But he clearly wasn't familiar with waterfowl apart from admiring strategically distant swans on manicured estates.

Droplet went for his head.

The ensuing chaos lasted for at least five gleeful minutes.
Droplet battered Lord Lengham as he attempted to hit her with

his magic—but he was an earth mage, they were three stories off the ground, and Lord Lengham didn't want to ruin his mansion. Droplet had no such qualms. As the battle entered the hallway, Lord Lengham called for his servants. None of them knew what to do with an enraged goose. In their confusion, Droplet fled into the house, toppling vases and ripping wall hangings, honking as she went.

When she was sure the whole house was actively pursuing her, she sped ahead, out of sight of the mob, and became a rat. These houses always had holes the owners didn't know about. She followed her nose into tunnels in the wall and attempted, in passing, to reassure the terrified rats that the galumphing of human and raptor feet would end soon.

The house still shook with chaos when Droplet found a way out. Droplet turned into a falcon and fled. She was victorious! She was the master of her fate! She could take on the world!

"You're grounded," Moss said.

"I'm twenty!" said Droplet.

"You're on kitchen duty for the next three months, at *minimum*," said Moss.

"Moss!"

"I support Moss entirely," said Nedrud as he valiantly attempted to keep a straight face. Rangitam and Moonshine had made no such attempt and were still howling with laughter on the other side of the room.

"And this human is going to be bringing us the records?" said Yelarcha. She looked fit to kill Droplet right there, but that look had grown less frightening over ten years of mutual cooperation and lack of murder.

"As many as he can carry. He knows what to bring us; he caught on quick. I think he could be a part of the team, even," Droplet said all in a rush. Yelarcha's murder gaze, if anything, intensified, but Nedrud looked thoughtful. Droplet continued, "He'll meet us in Elas Park at sundown."

" 'Us,' hm?" said Moss.

"You can't recognize him if I don't go with you," Droplet said sweetly.

Moss scowled.

"Devious youngster. Who raised you, hm?" said Nedrud, clapping Moss on the back with one of his giant paws.

Later, when the older adults couldn't hear, Moonshine whispered to Droplet, "Just like a real vigilante, huh? Awesome."

The dish duty would be worth it.

Forsyth met them at the park as planned. Droplet hadn't realized how many books a strong human in a panic could carry. He pulled them with him in a cart for this meeting.

"Now young one, I understand that you convinced Droplet here to take on your shape," said Moss.

"Yes, ma'am. And I understand that was a very big deal, and a very big secret, and I will never tell anyone about it," he said in a rush.

Moss nodded approvingly. "Droplet spoke highly of you," she said.

"Oh?" Forsyth said, surprised.

"She did. Makes me think you might even be interested in working with us on some...future projects."

Droplet looked at Moss in shock. She'd suggested this, of course, but she hadn't known the leaders would listen.

Forsyth didn't notice her astonishment. He looked like gold had fallen from the sky into his lap. "I would be honored, ma'am."

"Excellent. Let's talk more tomorrow, same time, same place. There's some people I want you to meet."

Chapter Eleven

Sacarus had its Eyes for keeping control within the city, but out of "the highest care for the safety of our illustrious residents and guests"—so said signs tacked by the road—patrols spread into the unincorporated countryside.

This was news to Azera.

"You didn't think to tell me we might be stopped and questioned?" she hissed to Droplet.

"I usually fly into the city! Or swim in! I don't bother with human things like this."

"I bother with human things! Human things bother with me!"

"You can't expect me to keep human things readily to mind, is all I'm saying."

"You're right. I don't know what I was thinking," Azera snapped. They sat in a grove of trees off the main road—the terrain had been almost entirely farmland and fallow fields for the past several miles. A hundred yards or so down the road, the flag of Makido flew over a large, featureless building built for strength. Beyond it, the river, the bay, and Sacarus waited, hazy in the distance. Travelers swarmed the road—tourists arriving for the midsummer festivities, no doubt.

"What kind of things will the military be checking for?" Droplet said. "How seriously do they take their jobs?"

"I don't know. I, unlike some people hiding in these trees, have never been here before!"

They continued in that vein. Perhaps, if Droplet had been

using senses besides a human's, she would have heard the guards approaching. But by the time she heard the *clink* of metal and the *crunch* of garzi feet, they were surrounded.

Three patrollers, humans in silver and red, flanked the grove. One woman spurred her garzi forward. "All right, hand it over," said the guard.

"Hand what over?" said Azera with a very convincing expression of confusion. Actually, she probably was confused. Droplet certainly was.

"Whatever it is you're talking about smuggling."

"We're not smuggling anything," Droplet protested.

"This is the only grove of trees for a mile around. The last hiding place before our outpost. You think this is our first day on the job?" the guard said.

"We just wanted a shady place to rest before we headed into Sacarus," Azera said. Convincing enough—the afternoon sun shone hot.

"I see," the guard said. "In that case, I'm sure you won't mind if we run a quick sensor over you to detect any contraband you may be carrying."

Droplet sighed and stood up. "What kind of sensor are we talking about?"

From her saddle, the guard produced a clear wand that shone white. "Nothing invasive. Picks up any particularly strong magic."

"There are a lot of legitimate reasons people could be carrying a powerful magical item," Droplet said. Her mind raced. Any kind of magical sensor would falter when it reached Azera.

"So you can tell us what those are. Innocent people have nothing to fear from this." She sounded deadpan, like she was reciting a dull lesson.

"Does that line ever actually reassure people?" Droplet said. But she stepped forward. She glanced at Azera, trying to be subtle about it; Azera was rubbing her wrists absently.

The guard dismounted and waved the wand perfunctorily across Droplet's body. It continued its pale white glow. "See, that wasn't so hard." The guard stepped over to Azera, who looked calm again. The guard waved the wand in the same casual way.

The light winked out.

The guard sighed. "How many bones are you hiding under there?"

"I'm cautious," Azera said. She forced a laugh. "No contraband, though."

"I'll need you to hand those bones over so we can check again," the guard said.

Azera's strained smile faltered.

"Is there a problem with that request?" said another guard from the back—an Air follower, and from vis fancier uniform, probably the captain.

"Uh," said Azera.

"They're the ones. Get them," the captain said.

"Wait, wha—?" Azera began, but fast as a striking snake, the guard next to her drew out a thin chain and whipped it around her hands. She yelped.

"What do you think you're doing?" Droplet snapped.

The captain raised an eyebrow at Droplet. Droplet spitefully wondered how many hours the captain had to spend practicing eyebrow raises to get the proper condescending effect.

"We're doing our job," the captain said. "Word came in last night that a necromancer and shapeshifter were causing mayhem in these parts. Now of course, the shapeshifter's description wouldn't be worth bunk, but I do believe that necromancer is said to look a lot like you," ve finished, turning to Azera.

Azera went blank. All emotion evaporated; her face settled into a neutral expression that terrified Droplet. "That's quite a coincidence," Azera said. She looked down at the coiled chain around her wrists, then at Droplet. She mouthed something that may have been "Run."

At the same time, one of the guards approached Droplet with a similar chain and said, "Don't try anything funny, shapeshifter."

Droplet wanted to laugh at them.

Humans.

She slowly untied the tether with the bone charm at her neck. She held it up. "Just a bone," she said to the suspicious guards, each with their respective wands and swords held at the ready. "Just a bone."

She let go.

And she became a roc.

Fabric tore around her and branches whipped around her head as she grew, golden feathers bursting from her skin. She screeched in pain from her wound being reshaped yet again, but the cry seemed to intimidate them: guards stumbled around and beneath her. Her feathered belly was as high off the ground as the tops of their heads. Infuriatingly, they had not fled in terror and were pre- paring to strike.

She hopped out of the grove, grabbing her bone pendant in one claw as she jumped, trying not to stumble. Tripping over trees would rather ruin the intimidating effect she was going for. She batted her wings, buffeting the guards with wind, and screeched once more. Azera, now entirely unguarded, stood rooted to the spot in awe, thus defeating the whole point of this. The chain around her hands had even gone slack, the other end dropped by the shocked guard. Droplet wished she could talk to the human.

If Azera wasn't going to run on her own, Droplet would need to pick her up and carry her.

The captain of the guard raised vis arms, shooting bands of crackling lightning through the air. Droplet raised the bone charm quickly, and the lightning aimed at her chest sparked into nothing- ness. Other beams passed by unaffected, though, and thin lines of pain needled through her outstretched wings.

Azera still wasn't running, damn it. Droplet took to the air. She heard screams. She had forgotten about the road—plenty of people going about their normal business had just seen a roc appear. Well, she wasn't going for subtle anyway.

She made a tight circle around the grove and the adjacent road, banking enough that her right wingtip nearly touched the ground while her left wingtip stretched twice as high as the treetops. She was attracting an audience—for every person on the road fleeing in terror, one stopped to stare.

This is why I need Moss, Droplet thought with some desperation. *She knows how to plan.*

Then a ghost appeared by her head.

"Young lady, I must admit I don't know where you're going with this," Azera's grandmother said.

You and me both, Droplet thought. She stopped circling to flap roughly in place. She wasn't sure whether a ghost could keep up with a circling roc.

"I thought perhaps you could carry Azera away? Screech once for yes."

Droplet screeched. She didn't see any downsides to evacuating as quickly as possible.

"Good woman. She'll be ready when you are."

Another burst of lightning from the ground dissipated harmlessly as it approached Azera's grandmother. A splinter shot off and hit Droplet's tail feathers, though. Droplet beat her wings hard, lifting herself higher. Azera, at long last, was backing away from the guards. She'd worked her hands out of the thin chain and carried both packs on her back. Droplet's roc eyesight was keen enough to make out her determined expression as she stared directly at Droplet.

Droplet banked sharply, flying around the tree grove as fast as her wings could carry her. The dragon-bone charm fell from her talons in her haste, but she couldn't stop for that. She slowed as she rounded; she had a clear shot at Azera, but she didn't want to hurt her.

Azera raised her arms above her head and scrunched her eyes shut. Droplet's right foot wrapped around almost her entire body, from her chest down to her ankles. Azera made a sound like "oof" as Droplet's foot hit. But nothing could be helped there—Droplet needed to keep up a quick enough speed to stay airborne.

With Azera secured, Droplet climbed and wheeled northwest.

The outpost building ahead swarmed like a disturbed anthill. Military poured through the doors and out of rooftop hatches.

Azera swore. As she summoned more assistance, the air under Droplet went cool.

Droplet had made many unsubtle escapes in her life, but this had to take the prize. The screams from the road merged with shouted orders and, soon, the muttering of disgruntled ghosts flying beneath her wings. Their presence did not help the screaming.

Droplet reached the riverbank and kept going at full speed. The river was nearly a mile wide at this point. She hoped the militia didn't have water patrols, though she wouldn't put it past them. The sounds of the chaos on the shore fell away. Below, boats rang bells and blew horns.

Veering right, Droplet headed toward the city. Azera yelped at the turn. In the calm, with no attack coming, Droplet began a descent, aiming for space amidst the boats on the river. Azera seemed to be muttering rapid prayers, but those were probably because of the pursuing Makidan officials on the bank. Probably.

As they approached the water, with it almost skimming Azera's toes, she called, "I can swim, so you know. Because I'm sure you were about to ask before plunging into a river."

Droplet had forgotten that humans couldn't all swim, but she wasn't about to admit that. Thankfully, she didn't have to. Instead, she dropped Azera and the bags.

The ghosts vanished.

Droplet turned into the Dalere human shape and fell, plummeting into frigid water that cut through this shape's minimal insulation. She swam back up, gasping as she broke the surface. Her first coherent thought was that Moss was going to kill her. She touched her bare chest ruefully and winced. At least the freshwater helped with that pain.

"I don't suppose, by chance, you have a plan?" Azera asked, treading water next to her as the current carried them along. Their bags bobbed beside them, floating lower and lower as the water soaked everything through.

"I'll help carry you to Sacarus. I can be a fish. Or a dolphin. Can the guards still see us?"

Azera looked pointedly over Droplet's shoulder at the bank. Dozens of uniformed Makidans lined the shore. Some had linked their arms to support what was sure to be a humdinger of a spell.

"You'd think they'd have something better to do with their time," Droplet said.

"You turned into a bird with talons longer than my legs," Azera said. "It was amazing, don't get me wrong, but can't you see why that would be, ah, intimidating?" She hooked her arms through the two packs to keep them from sinking entirely.

"I didn't hurt anyone," Droplet said.

"The blood mages could have said we hurt people," Azera said. Chanting echoed over the water. Boats veered away from them.

"Can you block whatever magic they're conjuring up?"

"Absolutely, but I'd rather not test it."

After a long, wet moment of mentally reviewing her aquatic forms, Droplet became a speckled river dolphin. Azera swam up to Droplet and clung to her stunted dorsal fin, placing herself between Droplet and the shore. With furious strokes of her dolphin tail, Droplet sped downstream.

Droplet recalled Harra's ridiculous dash down the docks. In comparison, that seemed like a model of planning and forethought.

If Sacarus was safety, something had gone horribly wrong.

The river widened and diverged around Sacarus as it flowed east. On the main island of Sacarus, thousands of people did the grunt work necessary to keep the rich in their perpetual bubble. The westernmost point did have a tree-filled park, though. Droplet could only hope that the copse had blocked their aerial getaway from the view of curious Sacarians and the city's Eyes. Even if it had, though, the city would hear the rumors soon enough.

Droplet kept her head underwater, echolocating as she went, the refractions of clicks forming a map of the river clearer than sight. She took the northern fork of the river so the bulk of the island would be between her and the shore she'd disturbed. She did her best to keep Azera's head above the river. Hopefully, Azera would shout if Droplet needed to know anything; a dolphin's eyes were lousy even when not in clouded water. At least echolocation would warn them of any purification spell-nets in the water. Even though Azera and her grandmother could nullify most magic, Droplet had no desire to run into one of those. Sure, mages said they were safe for river life and humans, but mages said a lot of things.

Soon after they passed the park, Azera called, "Here, here! Stop here!"

Droplet veered to her right through the murky water and clicked. A tiny set of steps, rounded by centuries of river currents, descended into the river. Droplet wedged her body against the steps so she wouldn't have to swim against the current, and Azera stumbled and slipped upward, dragging the soaking bags, at last finding her footing on dry cobblestones. She left a pool behind as she walked.

Droplet became a human—not the Dalere one. Too many people had seen that form now. But she couldn't be her noble Lady Kivak form either. She chose a stocky, curvy form with light-brown skin and long, straight black hair. This one had the advantage of not having any deity tattoos, so she could pose as any gender she needed to or forgo a gender altogether.

"Why did we stop?" she asked.

"Clotheslines," Azera said. She pointed. Sure enough, in this alleyway barely wide enough for two, rows over rows of clotheslines ascended to the sky. "If you're guiding us through the city, we need dry clothes."

"Good thinking," said Droplet. "Do you sense any magic?"

"Not a bit. But I don't know how fast the Eyes move."

"Too quickly," Droplet said. She climbed out of the water, leaving her own trail of puddles. At least the near-summer heat warmed her dripping skin.

Azera pulled down a couple of white shirts and deep-green pants from the lines. "Servant stuff. Best way to go unnoticed."

"I know that, but why do you know that?" Droplet asked.

"Oh, Harra—" Azera turned to Droplet, yelped, squeezed her eyes shut, and spun away, still holding out a shirt and pants.

"Humans are so weird about nudity," Droplet said, taking the clothes. "You've seen me naked before!"

"That was different! You're different now!"

"Is there something wrong with this body?" Droplet asked, perplexed.

"No! Nothing is wrong at all! That's the problem!"

Droplet tilted her head to one side, staring at Azera's averted form. Water plopped onto stone. Finally, the realization clicked. "OH. Humans, I swear..."

"Just put some clothes on," Azera muttered, embarrassed.

"Let's get some extras to dry with first."

Azera nodded and set the dry clothes aside as she looked for the most-absorbent options.

"So, Harra?" Droplet prompted.

"Right. Harra's a maid, you know, and she told me all about it. And I've seen it myself—Harra helped sneak me in at the parties with the best food whenever there was enough left over to go around the household staff. You wouldn't believe the sordid stuff Harra heard while she worked. Or maybe you would," Azera added. She grabbed a shirt. Droplet reached for one, too, and Azera cut in, "Not that, the fabric is hellish to wash. We want to make things as easy as possible on the people who have to clean up after us here."

Droplet had rarely been on laundry duty at the organization. She stepped back to defer to Azera's knowledge.

"Anyway, Harra makes most of her money selling the gossip to *Mage Life* and *High Society Weekly*, and nobody's ever suspected her." Azera selected a shirt full of stains, even after washing, and handed it backward over her shoulder, still avoiding looking at Droplet.

"Clever. I like her," Droplet declared, accepting the shirt. She made a mental note to suggest this to Moss as a new line of revenue for the organization.

"She's very clever. The upper crust are also very oblivious," Azera said, sighing. "I didn't understand how oblivious until I started courting one of them, of course. All right, are you looking away? I've got to change."

Droplet rolled her eyes but turned away, drying herself and changing. Clothing rustled behind her as Azera did the same. Droplet wanted to ask more about Azera's oblivious ex-fiancée but restrained herself. It wasn't relevant to the mission. Plus, she *had* dropped Azera in a river less than an hour ago, and Azera probably had limits to how much suffering she would tolerate at Droplet's hands in such a short time.

Nobody had been so kind as to leave sandals out to dry. Fishing around in her waterlogged bag, Droplet found an extra pair of her own. She put them on, sodden as they were. They didn't fit these feet, pinching in the front and loose in the back. But it would be better than being barefoot. Azera, of course, still had her own soggy sandals. They spread out their makeshift towels on the ground and tucked some of their money into the pockets—three times more than the simple clothes were actually worth, to cover the inconvenience. Dressed, damp, with soaking packs on their backs, they squelched out of the alleyway and into Sacarus.

With servant's clothes and the other essential component of the disguise—a determined, purposeful expression—Droplet was confident that nobody would look at them twice on the street. Certainly not closely enough to wonder about their still-wet hair and shoes. The outside of the packs already looked almost dry in the hot sun.

In Sacarus, though, the people weren't the only ones watching.

The Eyes of the City were not *everywhere, all the time*—much as the island enforcers would like them to be. But at any moment, a black-ink sketch of an eye could appear on any wall in the city, facing in or out. Watching.

Azera and Droplet had talked about it on the road.

"Can they recognize *everyone?*" Azera had asked.

"Nobody's figured that out. We tried. There have to be people watching through the drawings somehow, and if people are involved, they may make mistakes...but we don't know what kind of people, so we can't guess what kind of mistakes they make."

"Will they know that we're new?"

"Probably. We won't have a home to go to, and they watch visitors more closely than most residents."

Now, entering the city for the first time in years, Droplet had to contemplate another urgent question: did the patrols send descriptions of fugitives to the mysterious humans behind the Eyes? Could the blood mages have given a tip to the Eyes directly?

Probably. Not only because it would make sense for those forces to cooperate but also because that would be *just their luck.*

Azera and Droplet squished deeper into the city.

The gray and red stone buildings of the main island of Sacarus had stood, mostly unchanged, for centuries. Homes, churches, grocers, butchers, moneychangers, and all the other necessities of life had been plopped down seemingly at random. With few exceptions, Sacarus did not have streets so much as connected gaps between buildings. Some lasted only the length of a red-and-gray temple front, and at the longest, they ran for a quarter mile. Droplet chose turns that kept them moving east and north.

Their footsteps echoed in the emptiness.

"Where *is* everyone?" Azera muttered.

"Working, I guess. You'll see plenty of people once we have to cross over the Resplendent Promenade."

"The Resplendent Promenade? Really?"

"Really. But all the natives call it Hell Street."

"That's not any more reassuring."

"Honestly, if we can make it there before the Eyes see us, it will be the best luck we've had this whole trip."

"Great. Let's hurry up and get to Hell Street," Azera said with a disbelieving laugh.

"You could have stayed home."

Azera only snorted, as if that option was too ridiculous to consider.

The Resplendent Promenade cut a wide diagonal from the southwestern side of the island, where the main bridge to Makido stood, all the way to the far northeast corner of the crescent. At those docks, the ships of the wealthy disembarked for the smaller islands.

Almost every visitor to this city built for visitors had to pass through the Resplendent Promenade.

Turning the corner from empty, gray-walled alleys onto the

Promenade, Droplet felt like Hell Street surely had to hold half the people in the whole known world. Humans, raptors, hybrids, even griffins jostled for space. Every building façade boasted of wealth and power. A single mosaic depicting the victory of the guardians covered an Elasian temple front; a temple to the Air Deity directly opposite featured another full-front mosaic backed in gold. A store with windows of shimmering gold and jewels—"Finest Spells Money Can Buy: Fortune, Love, Protection"—had sprung for a *full waterfall* down the three-story building frontage, the water parting artfully for the window displays and plunging at last into a miniature moat. Occasional gusts of floral perfume, frying seafood, and ripe citrus cut through the stench of hundreds of sweaty people. Banners hung from houses, from stalls, from poles held by enterprising people who shouted about the most lucrative gambling den, the fastest garzi races, the widest variety of crossbows, and so much more.

"And I thought Ninuthen took the prize for unnecessary magic," Azera muttered, eyeing one façade covered in a shimmering illusion of shooting stars against the night sky. She rubbed her arms uneasily as she and Droplet wound their way through the throng. The magic must have been prickling against her constantly.

The barrage on the senses continued until, within sight of the docks, Droplet turned south. Only a few buildings away from Hell Street—and as many turns around corners—the hubbub faded to a distant roar, like the sound of waves from over dunes. Droplet stole a glance at Azera; she seemed dazed, as if she'd been hit over the head.

"So that's Hell Street right before midsummer," said Droplet.

"I need to lie down," Azera said.

Droplet had a keen sense of direction, but she hadn't been in Sacarus for many years. She led Azera through a few overlapping squares and zigzags of gray stone that *all looked the same* before at last turning onto the equally unremarkable street where Rangitam Stelson lived.

She stopped cold. An Eye watched across from Rangitam's door. The thick, rough black lines looked like they'd been scrawled with an angry brush.

Droplet took a deep breath. "Act normal," she muttered to Azera, who had stopped behind her out of necessity.

Azera didn't respond; hopefully the human had understood. Droplet resumed walking toward the door.

The irregular pupil of the Eye slid left until the drawing looked straight at her.

She knocked on the door of Rangitam's house as the old lessons she'd learned about living in Sacarus came flooding back. *Don't act like you have something to hide. If possible, keep doing what you were doing when you saw the Eye. Don't stare at the Eye.*

She prayed to the Sea Goddess that the Eye didn't have Azera's description yet.

A half-dog wearing the Earth God's sigil around his neck opened the door. Patches of red and white fur covered his head, hands, and tail, and he raised his floppy ears as he took in the visitors. His gaze rested only for the briefest second on the Eye outside the door.

"May I help you?" he asked.

"Are you Rangitam Stelson?" Droplet asked, knowing full well that he was. He looked healthy, and she felt calmer, instantly, see-ing her old friend and mentor.

"I am, but I don't believe I have the pleasure of your acquain-tance," he said. His ears and tail drooped.

"You knew my father, and you would have seen me when I was much smaller," Droplet said, trying and failing to smile. Af-ter all these years, the need for misdirection and omission of key truths came naturally enough, but she hadn't expected an Eye to be right at her back, testing for loopholes. "My father is Lareme

Downharbor." A painfully common Makidan name, and thus a code name for the organization members and some trusted allies. The Lareme Downharbors of the world hopefully remained in blissful ignorance of their involvement in dozens of missions to tear down the wealthy.

"Old Lareme! How is he? Come in, come in," said Rangitam, ears and tail back to chipper. He ushered them through the doorway, which was quite a squeeze. As Droplet's ear passed under his head—she was as short as Azera in this form, goodness—he muttered, "Fake it for as long as you can; we'll go elsewhere when we bring up lodging."

"Got it," Droplet muttered back, then said in a normal voice, "Lareme's doing great—he misses you, of course." She'd talk about Moss in place of this Lareme. That would be the easiest lie.

Rangitam led them into a tiny sitting room of threadbare furniture. He'd lined most of the walls with bookshelves, and Azera's shoulders relaxed a fraction. Books dampened magic, so perhaps they'd be extra soothing for a necromancer. The stucco walls had some simple vines painted on them. Droplet saw a small Eye stationed among the leaves and dropped her gaze.

Azera rose to the occasion as soon as Rangitam turned to her. She kept asking questions about his life—Droplet had to admire her skills at asking "How's the weather been? What's it like living on an island full of tourists? That must make trips to the market difficult!" It wasn't only a love of small talk.

She must have spent so much of her life trying to keep people from looking at her too closely, Droplet thought.

Rangitam offered them tea with an air of relief. From occasional far-speak conversations, Droplet knew that he'd built a wide network of casual allies here in his endeavor to rebuild the organization's work. He probably got a lot of visitors who couldn't lie to save their own skins.

After nearly a half hour, Rangitam asked where they'd be

staying.

Droplet and Azera exchanged a glance.

"We haven't figured that out yet," Droplet said.

"Let me take you over to the Ganlians' church."

"You have Ganlians here?" Azera said in shock.

"Oh, they love us here," Rangitam said with a laugh. "Best supply of afflicted heathens the world can offer. But the beds are clean, and they serve a hell of a breakfast. I'll show you there."

Chapter Twelve

Ganlians, followers of the Phoenix Child, thought magic was a sin, the lure of the devil—and they only had one devil, which seemed insufficient to Droplet. Ganlians devoted themselves to ridding the world of magic's corruption.

This wasn't going well for them.

But up against the entire panoply of what magic could offer a person, Ganlians had one key weapon in their arsenal: offering cheap lodging and good food at all times, no questions asked.

Rangitam led them to the Church of the Constant Fire. It sat on the northern side of Hell Street, only a block back from the hub-bub. Though its walls were stained dark gray by layers of grime, the bowl of flame above the door burned bright, a beacon in the twilight blue. Hundreds of tiny panels of carved bone adorned the heavy wooden doors. A wrinkled Ganlian priestess with a shock of curly white hair welcomed them with open arms, literally.

"What a good day this is, bringing new visitors to our door! Welcome, welcome. I'm Mother Enneth. Come on in." Mother—that would be a "she" for Ganlians, then. Droplet had never gotten the hang of figuring out proper forms of address for people who didn't follow the First Four and the god-tokens system. Once the heavy door had thudded shut behind them, Mother Enneth asked, "And what are your names? Do I get real names with these ones?" she added to Rangitam.

"That's up to them, ma'am," said Rangitam.

Mother Enneth sighed. "The only fair response, I suppose." She returned her attention to the bewildered Droplet and Azera. "What names would you like me to use while you're here, dears?"

"Are...are you actually a priestess?" said Azera.

"I'm a priestess, and despite what many seem to think about Ganlians, that word is not a synonym for 'fool,'" Mother Enneth said dryly. "For instance, when someone spends a few years bringing all their visitors to a friendly, welcoming, warded building without a single Eye, it doesn't take me a few years to figure things out."

"It's the breakfasts, Mother. Your people do things with sausages and eggs that are almost enough to convert me," said Rangitam, face the picture of sincerity.

"Flatterer."

"I'm Azera."

"Dalere."

Dozens of nooks for bone carvings of phoenixes and saints pockmarked the scrubbed, off-white walls of the church. No Eye was getting in here.

"How long will you need a room for?" Mother Enneth asked.

"That's one of the many things we wish we knew," Azera said.

"Let's say until the day after the solstice," Droplet said.

Azera looked shocked. "That's remarkably optimistic, from you," she said.

"You're a bad influence," Droplet said.

"One bed will have to be enough. There's always an influx of people seeking shelter around the solstice," Mother Enneth said. She grimaced, though Droplet couldn't tell whether the displeasure came from the overabundance of people or from other, darker thoughts. Hopefully just the crowds. They certainly were enough to perturb Droplet.

They'd arrived as dinner was ending. They snagged bowls of flaky white fish (for Azera and Rangitam) and a concoction of nuts, vegetables, and dried fruits (for all three), and then Mother Enneth led them to a clean-yet-drab room with a threadbare rug in faded reds, oranges, and yellows and a scratched wooden flame icon on the wall. A shelf in the washstand by the table held a battered copy of the *Lanren*, the Ganlians' holy book. The bed smelled of fresh straw, which must have been hard to come by here on the island. The Ganlians really did look out for their visitors.

Once Mother Enneth had left, Azera, Droplet, and Rangitam could, for the first time, talk freely.

"Rangitam, it's Moss's Droplet," Droplet said.

"Sport!" He embraced her. She had *not* been expecting that; she went stiff at the unexpected contact. He had the grace to not comment on that or on her continued use of "Droplet." "You made it! Oh, thank the gods, Moss and I have been worried sick. I'll tell her you're safe as soon as I return home. Tell me about your journey— tell me about your life! How's Moss? We chat, of course, but it's so hard to get real news with the Eyes watching..."

Droplet assured Rangitam of Moss's health and told him more about their missions in Ninuthen. With Azera's help, she filled him in on their current trip. Rangitam woofed softly at their tale.

"The blood mages could be anywhere," he said. "For anyone else, I'd say the big island was out of the question, but blood mages would have enough power to deal with the Eyes."

"Would they want to, though? They *do* have to shed blood every time they want to do magic," said Droplet.

"They don't have to shed *their* blood," Rangitam said darkly. Azera put her face in her hands, and he hurriedly backtracked. "But they usually do! It's hard to get willing blood from other people! They save that for the really important stuff!"

"I don't think that's helping," Droplet murmured, leaning closer to Rangitam. His ears drooped. He looked over Azera and Droplet, then sniffed the air.

"Why don't you both get rest? You've had a trying few days. A rest in a real bed will do you good."

"When blood mages could be taking Harra's memories even as

we speak?" said Azera. He whimpered, and she held up a hand to stop him. "I know, I know. I'm not going anywhere right now. I can't." She sighed and slumped, her disappointment in her body's insistence on having limits plain on her face.

"I hate to say it, but there's only so much we can do without rest," Droplet said.

"You really have been listening to Moss," Rangitam said, impressed.

"Maybe tomorrow, we won't almost die. Can we try for that?" Azera said.

"I can't make any promises," said Droplet.

Azera nodded in resignation.

When Rangitam had left, Droplet slumped to the ground, pillowing her head on her arms. Everything hurt. Azera flopped onto her back on the bed with an enthusiastic sigh. The room was comfortably warm, and the stone kept out the worst of the summer's heat. The two rested in silence. Despite a growing numbness in Droplet's right arm, she didn't move a muscle.

Mother Enneth found them like that five minutes later. She seemed to be suppressing a laugh.

"Is there anything I can get you?" she asked.

"A change of clothes, if you have any spares, and a line to dry things on," Azera said. Their bags' contents were still wet from the soaking in the river.

"I don't suppose you have any paliot leaves?" said Droplet.

"Oh, we always keep those on hand."

"Really?!" Droplet raised her head.

"When you shelter all comers, no questions asked, you prepare for all sorts of things," Mother Enneth said.

After Mother Enneth had dropped off the clothes and paliot leaves, Droplet stood up like she was pulling continents with each limb. Out of respect for the human's peculiar ways, she faced away from Azera as she disrobed. The chill of the paliot leaves was less bitter today. Despite her best efforts, the burn was actually healing. "You should get the bed tonight," Azera said. Droplet looked back over her right shoulder. Azera's eyes were closed, but she was sitting up from the straw mattress with obvious reluctance.

"Absolutely not. I'm trying to look out for you."

"You dropped me in a river."

"It seemed like the best option at the time."

"It probably was. Congratulations! Take the bed," said Azera, waving an arm (accidentally saying **Look behind the beehive, angry cow** in the process).

"I've slept on floors before."

"So have I."

"You need to rest and recover," said Droplet.

"So do you. I'm not going to be out-martyred by you, damn it," she said.

"Fine, fine," Droplet grumbled. "Neither of us gets to be martyrs tonight. We'll share the bed."

"Oh," Azera said, her voice suddenly much higher pitched.

"Budge over. We'll both fit."

"Is that the best idea?"

"You don't want me to be a martyr, I don't want you to be a martyr, so we're going to suffer the indignity of sharing a bed, and that's final," Droplet said. She nudged Azera's leg.

Azera still hadn't moved or opened her eyes. "You didn't put a shirt on, did you," she said.

Droplet sighed. Humans! "I'll get under one of the blankets so I don't offend your delicate sensibilities. I'm trying not to get paliot paste all over the shirt I intend to wear tomorrow."

"We can probably get another if we need it. Mother Enneth seems very well-supplied," said Azera. With eyes still squeezed shut, she groped for the edge of the bed, rolling as far toward the wall as she could, until she was lying on her right side with her nose nearly pressed to the stone. Droplet snuffed the oil lamp and, as promised, climbed in and under the blanket.

I can still be a martyr, putting on a blanket in this warmth, she thought. "You're safe now from the horror of looking at an appealing unclothed human."

"Droplet!" said Azera.

Droplet hadn't known that a tone of voice could blush, but she learned something new every day. Night. With a self-satisfied noise, she closed her eyes. The poky straw mattress felt soft as clouds. She basked in the sensation, sure she would be asleep in a minute.

In less than a minute, Azera spoke again. "You and Rangitam go way back, then," she said.

Droplet silently asked the Sea Goddess for fortitude. "I met him when I was very young. Him and the other founding members of the organization."

"Like Moss?" Azera asked.

"Moss was a founding member, but she was still living with my colony when I was born. She's always liked the cities, but she wanted to be around for my birth."

"Is she a relative?"

"My other parent."

"Your *parent*? She'd better have stuck around for your birth, if she's your parent! Neither of you said anything," Azera said, wonderingly.

"It's different for shapeshifters," Droplet said. "The one who fathers the child doesn't have to be a parent. It all depends on what the mother wants. Some parents don't even know they've fathered a child, if the mother is the more solitary type, like a tiger. My mother and Moss are both very social—like humans, you know, you all need your people around to be healthy."

"I suppose that's true," Azera said. She rolled onto her back. A few inches of space remained between them still. "So what happened to you?" she asked. Droplet made a strangled noise in her throat. "It's late. I'm too tired to be polite about it. You grew up in a big community, you call yourself a goose, both your parents like company..."

Droplet sighed. She fiddled with the edge of the blanket as she thought. Here in the dark, when she couldn't see the real world, when her body and mind felt wrung out, talking felt easier. All the reasons for secrecy and reticence fell away and left behind no defense against the wish for a real companion.

"I've been doing this a long time. I guess you could say I was an apprentice to Moss and Rangitam and their friends," Droplet said. "We've done all sorts of work to help out shapeshifters and hybrids—mostly shapeshifters and hybrids. Some humans, some raptors, some griffins. We've taken down a lot of rich, powerful humans and raptors in the process. It's scary work. We kept adding new people to the organization for most of my time there—all sorts of people. All kinds of species, including humans. There were dozens of us." Even though humans and raptors were on top of society, there were still many humans and raptors beneath, in pain, powerless. They wanted to fight back.

Droplet went silent for so long that Azera nudged her with her elbow through the blanket. "I'm awake. I'm awake." It still took her a long time to answer. "The humans and raptors always left. They always had something else they cared about more than us. I don't know how many apologies I've heard now about how they can't do this anymore because Little Timanthemum needs them alive. As if we wouldn't take care of their children. As if we *weren't* taking care of everyone's kids, constantly. I spent so many years of my life babysitting, you have no idea."

"I wish I could have seen that," Azera said.

"I'm so glad you didn't. I'm trying to make a reputation as a fearless vigilante, now."

"Your secret's safe with me." Azera yawned. She shuffled to get more comfortable, and her arm came to rest against Droplet's through the blanket. Droplet didn't mention it. "In seriousness, that's tough. I can see why you'd become suspicious."

"Oh, I didn't finish. I got distracted remembering the babysitting years."

Azera tensed. "What happened?"

"Four years ago, in Panithen, a human sold us out," said Droplet. Azera gasped. "We scattered after that. The ones who made it out. We couldn't stay together and escape—too obvious. Moss and I have spent those years in Nortak. Rangitam's been here. A couple others went to Owl's Point. And some people...most people... vanished."

Azera rolled toward Droplet and placed a hand on her bare shoulder. Droplet found herself thinking of how she'd tried to comfort Azera. Gods, a hand on a shoulder was feeble comfort, wasn't it? She reached up and placed a hand over Azera's, intending to push her off, but instead just...left her hand there, holding Azera's. *Useless.* She squeezed, ever so slightly, as she tried not to tear up.

Azera rubbed her shoulder. "Thank you for telling me," she whispered, then yawned hugely. As Droplet tried to form a response, silence bloomed between them. The days had been long, the night was dark, and the bed was soft and warm. Every sentence she tried to construct ran away from her consciousness half-formed. The last thing Droplet heard was Azera murmuring, on the edge of sleep herself, "You don't have to trust me, then. I understand."

Droplet woke up rested and comfortable. This was such an unexpected feeling that she was immediately suspicious. She opened her eyes and saw Azera's face inches from her own. The necromancer slept soundly, face slack as she snored.

At some point in the night, Azera's arm had flopped over her, though the blankets were still between them. Even relaxed, the muscles stood out. *Carpentry does wonders for a human's appearance,* Droplet thought idly.

Stars. She really needed to get out of bed.

Droplet attempted to scoot out from under Azera's arm, misjudged the width of the bed, and fell to the floor, taking the blanket with her.

"Ow!"

"AAAH!" Azera screamed. Droplet sat up, confused. Azera blinked at her, then shut her eyes. "Uh. Sorry. Reflex?"

"What the stars kind of reflex is that?"

"It's been a weird few days, Droplet," Azera said through gritted teeth, eyes still closed.

"You can look at me," Droplet said, exasperated. "I'm not averting my eyes from your bare arms or anything."

"Are bare arms particularly...uh...special for shapeshifters?"

"What? No, that's silly. I'm saying you have attractive arms, and you don't see me ceasing to function every time I lay eyes on them," Droplet said, and instantly regretted saying it.

Azera opened her eyes and fixed them firmly on Droplet's face. She frowned at what she saw. "You're serious?"

Oh well, can't take it back now... "Yes, clearly."

"My ex-fiancée made me hide my arms every time we went somewhere together. She said they showed I did work with my hands."

"Your ex-fiancée had no taste," said Droplet.

Azera groaned and rolled onto her back, closing her eyes once more as she sprawled. "I do not *cease to function* when I'm uncomfortable," she muttered.

"If you wanted 'comfortable,' you should have stayed home," Droplet grumbled.

Azera stiffened. "This again?"

"What? I'm just saying, you didn't have to come."

"And I thought we covered this already? Especially 'cause I've saved your neck, what, twice now?"

"From situations I wouldn't have *been* in if I'd come alone," said
Droplet.

"No, you would have been in other situations!" Azera sat up,
opening her eyes again and glaring.

"Situations where I wasn't trying to save a human—" Droplet
said, closing the gap between her and the edge of the bed, the better to loom.

"Oh yeah, you're the big bloody hero, always the savior, every
time?" Azera snapped, sitting up on her knees so she matched
Droplet's height.

"About time you—"

"You aren't the only one who can save people!"

Droplet paused. And stars, that pause was an awful decision,
because she stopped to look at Azera's eyes, and face, and her half-
open mouth—no, no, back to the human's eyes.

"You have some skills that will come in handy when we rescue
Harra. I admit it," she said, stiffly.

"I'm not only talking about Harra, you fool," said Azera.

This was too much. Droplet whirled away from the human to
grab a shirt. She pulled it over her head.

Azera didn't stop talking. "Maybe those first two times I saved
your ungrateful skin don't count, sure. Even if I grant you that,
when we've found the blood mages, you're not just going to look
out for me. I'm going to look out for you too. Because that's what
happens when you work together," Azera snapped. When Droplet didn't answer, Azera continued, softer, "Did you really think I
would pull you into this and abandon you?"

"Yes!" Droplet said.

Azera didn't get a chance to reply because Mother Enneth
knocked on the door to tell them breakfast was being served and
Rangitam was there. Droplet bolted out the door, and if the human
said anything else, she didn't hear it. She told herself the funny
feeling in her stomach was hunger. To be fair, when the smell of

fresh-baked bread hit her nose, her stomach *did* make its hunger painfully known.

One day left until the solstice. Only one day. She could make it through that.

Rangitam had far-spoken with Nedrud and Moss during the night. Neither sent helpful news, but both had asked him to pass on their love and their appreciation that Droplet was not dead. That morning, Rangitam arrived at the church with a rolled-up map of the island, a couple more changes of clothes, and some spare money. He assured Droplet that he had plenty more, that Nedrud would be happy it was going to good use, and that Nedrud had asked for a report on how these clothes compared to her Makidan robe.

Breakfast at the Church of the Constant Flame was everything Rangitam had promised. Dark, soft, rich bread with butter and honey, some kind of pie filled with fluffy eggs and summer vegetables, half a dozen juices, and more. The sausage smelled good enough to make Droplet wish she ate cooked meat. Every room of the common areas was packed, and breakfasters spilled into the hallways. Droplet did have to field a few inquiries from nuns about whether she'd be attending the service after breakfast, but she was full enough and rested enough to be polite as she rebuffed them.

Over breakfast, Rangitam kept up small talk with Droplet and Azera. He'd obviously noticed the tension, though he said nothing direct about it. As Droplet and Azera both ate their fill, much of the tension dissipated, leaving—at least for Droplet—the bitter aftertaste of *oh gods and stars, I really said that?*

But she could work through the regret of saying too much. She had lots of practice.

After breakfast, when most of the people had vanished—perhaps they'd been less averse to the offered service—Rangitam rolled out his map. He noted the alarm on Droplet's face and said, "It's okay, everyone still here is doing something suspicious."

Droplet checked for herself. Indeed, the dozen-odd griffins, humans, hybrids, and raptors left in the room all huddled over their breakfast tables and talked in soft voices. And everyone wore bland, unremarkable clothing—except for those who wore one or two eye-catching, easily removable accessories. One griffin wore an ostentatiously sparkly clip of the Air Deity's sigil on ver crown feathers, and a human kept fiddling with a blocky red necklace with a flimsy clasp.

"Not to make light of foreign gods, especially ones sheltering us from the law, but what exactly do the Phoenix Child's followers believe in besides the evil of magic?" Azera asked.

"That's a question for Mother Enneth," said Rangitam.

Sacarus claimed a few dozen islands throughout its lagoon. Except for a couple islands necessary to civic functioning—the cemetery and the dump—the islands housed the wealthy and powerful. Some had themes, like the Lily Island, the Coral Island, and the Island of Masks, and were open to whoever could pay. Others were private homes. General consensus held that to be invited to a private home carried far more prestige than attending an island one only had to pay money to attend. Practically common, that.

"The cultists have to be on one of the private islands, or anyone could show up," said Droplet.

"That rules out about a third of them," said Rangitam. "And some of the private ones are too busy or small for anyone to be hiding a cult..." He leaned over the table and began ticking little "X"s beside islands. Most of the islands had "X"s by them, in different pen colors and thicknesses, many faded nearly to nothing. She envied a person who could hold on to a useful object for more than one mission.

Rangitam paused after finishing his markings, frowning at the map. Eleven islands remained. Droplet let the silence stretch for a minute before saying, "I was hoping you'd have a lot more criteria to toss out."

"Nothing as easy as that." Rangitam huffed. "I can make guesses, given what I know of the private owners, but only guesses. It's harder to infiltrate the territory of the rich without a dedicated team." Droplet slumped. Rangitam looked sideways at her. "Now Mother Enneth...she knows quite a bit about the city. I think she could be very useful."

Droplet straightened up again and glared at him. He gave her a pleading, puppy-dog-eyed look, which was entirely unfair. "I see what you're doing. You're trying to get me to agree to a full recruit," she accused, though not with the same venom she might have used before he gave her those pleading eyes.

"We need to start rebuilding, Droplet. It's been years."

"And you're not merely planning to recruit—you want to recruit more people whose first loyalty won't be to the organization."

"Think of how many more people we could save if we got back up to our full strength!"

"Think of how many more people we'll lose," Droplet shot back. His ears drooped. He was still using those dog eyes on her, dang it. She sighed and rubbed her head. She didn't want to yell at Rangitam. He was family in everything but blood. "We can use Mother Enneth for this job without telling her the whole story. I'll leave the bigger picture here in Sacarus up to you and Nedrud."

Rangitam nodded. He tried not to smile, but she could feel the breeze of his tail wagging under the seat. He'd always been terrible at bluffing in card games.

They gave Mother Enneth a mostly true story: the Cult of the Endless War had stolen Azera's dear friend Harra; Droplet (Dalere), another Ninuthen resident, had agreed to help Azera get Harra back; and Rangitam was an old friend of Dalere's parents. Mother Enneth embraced Azera to console her, which did seem to comfort Azera.

The Mother showed no surprise that a notorious cult of blood mages was operating out of Sacarus.

"Did you know they were here?" Azera asked.

"There are rumors—always rumors—but not enough to be certain. How many people has the cult taken?" Mother Enneth asked.

That, they didn't know. The four of them did some estimates and math, scrawling notes on a tattered corner of Rangitam's map. If Droplet had seen three crates prepared, and one successful kidnapping...if Azera had heard of five kidnappings, or maybe six, she wasn't sure...if the blood cultists struck this many cities this often...

At the end, they had a range of anywhere from 20 to 50 likely captives.

"Oh, that's great!" Rangitam said.

"That's...great?" Azera echoed.

"That's enough people to leave a lot of evidence no matter how careful the blood mages are," Droplet said.

"Exactly. You would not believe how hard it is to track down a single missing person, even if you know who took them," Rangitam said.

Droplet shuddered, remembering years and missions past.

Mother Enneth smiled at them. "I see you're old hands at this sort of thing. Or I would see, of course, if I wasn't an innocent, elderly Ganlian who tragically can never quite remember these sorts of details when pressed by Sacarian officers."

Droplet glowered.

"Old hands at this, perhaps, but not at Sacarus. That's where your wisdom comes in, oh bestower of bountiful breakfasts," said Rangitam.

Mother Enneth raised her walking stick in the air, and an acolyte came running over.

"Yes, Mother?"

"Could you fetch me some pillows, dear? I'll be helping these
folks for quite some time, and my bones need some comfort."

Once Mother Enneth and the acolyte had sufficiently arranged
an armful of pillows, she continued. "As I see it, we've got two
fronts to work on. One is hearsay and rumor. We figure out what
everyone's seen and heard, and we see if we can piece it together
without getting caught. The other is the Sacarian Port Authority
Records."

An island city as tightly controlled as Sacarus, with so many
powerful visitors to appease, kept meticulous shipping records.
Droplet hoped they'd kept better track of their records than the
slapdash job nobility made of it in other cities. She could have hap-
pily gone the rest of her life without revisiting the resigned dread
of impending high-stakes boredom. She caught Rangitam's gaze on
her and sighed.

Azera and Mother Enneth looked at her in some confusion.

Oh, right. New people.

"I'll visit the records," Droplet said.

"Dalere will know what to look for," said Rangitam to the humans at the table.

Mother Enneth frowned. "Have the Eyes not seen you yet?"

"I'm...good at disguises," Droplet said. She still had one more
human form in reserve. Well, two if she was desperate...but no,
better to treat that last form as useless.

"And let me guess, you're planning to go alone?" Azera said.

Droplet met Azera's gaze and saw fire there. "Yes." Droplet held
Azera's gaze for a few moments before adding, "You, Rangitam, and
Mother Enneth can track down other leads while I read through
the records. We'll move faster that way. And you're much better
than me at talking to people."

Azera didn't look any happier, but she nodded. That was something, at least.

"What does Dalere need to know about the records office?" Rangitam asked.

After a thorough briefing by Mother Enneth and a close look at the map, Droplet left the table for the secret back exit. Because of course this house of worship had a secret back exit. She'd barely gone ten steps down the hallway when she heard Azera following. She sighed and turned.

Azera looked uncomfortable. This did not make Droplet feel any more positive about the odds of the coming conversation being a good one.

"Listen, about this morning and last night," Azera said.

Droplet scanned the hallway, but they were alone. "You...have been helpful. I may have said some things I didn't totally, completely, wholeheartedly mean," she allowed, shifting from foot to foot. Her cheeks heated up.

"I meant all of what I said," said Azera.

"Oh," Droplet said, and gods, she was going to melt from blushing. This was the worst thing that had happened to her today. Granted, it was barely past breakfast, but still.

"You don't have to trust me. But I'll be looking out for you anyway, whether you like it or not. That's all."

Droplet nodded slowly. After a pause, she said, "So you aren't here to yell at me for going off alone?"

"Apparently, sometimes, you barging off on your own is the best plan we have," Azera grumbled.

"Only sometimes?" Droplet said.

"I don't think we're very good at plans yet."

Yet.

Droplet could see too much of a future in that "yet." So she left.

Chapter Thirteen

Summerbird visited Panithen once or twice a year, usually un-announced. "Mail from the mountains" was a Panithen idiom for slow and unreliable, and far-speak discs were costly. So when Droplet, at age 25, received a letter from her mother, her first reaction was alarm.

She read the letter in her bedroom, the one she shared with Moonshine. Moonshine found her there half an hour later, lying on her back in her original human form, gazing at the ceiling.

Moonshine, in lynx form, hopped onto the bed. **What is it?** she asked.

"A letter from Mother," said Droplet.

Summerbird? Really?

"Read it," Droplet said, waving the paper toward Moonshine. Moonshine gave the paper a disdainful look and shifted to her in-born human appearance: a short, pale form with a button nose. Both Droplets had now honored more allied humans with their forms over the years, but they tried not to use those forms. The humans' understanding of the honor did not quite outweigh, as Forsyth put it, the "gut creepiness" that someone could be walking around wearing your shape at any time.

" 'My little Droplet,' " Moonshine read, " 'Wonderful news! Our colony met another during the winter migration, and now I know half a dozen people ready to map the seas. We are planning the voyage already. I will come to you in some months when we are ready. Root of the Tallest Tree sends her love and asks you to send more of those flaky, sweet pastries—' "

"You can stop there. The rest is all little updates like that," said Droplet. Moonshine put the letter down. She joined Droplet on the bed, sitting cross-legged, and looked down at Droplet's face.

"The sea, huh," Moonshine said.

"It makes sense. I mean, it's the highest calling, right? Finding all there is to know..." Droplet trailed off.

"Our moms have always been traditional. Really believe in the star-walkers and all that stuff." Moonshine's mother had left years ago on a similar expedition past the northern shore, to the uncounted islands dotting the arctic seas. Moonshine received intermittent letters, usually written six months to a year before their arrival and sent from tiny villages with names in languages nobody in the house recognized.

"Hey, *I* believe in the star-walkers too," said Droplet.

"Mhmm. Going to join your mom and go explore the deep ocean, then?" Moonshine challenged.

"You know I'm not," Droplet snapped. "But this means I have to tell Mom that."

"Oof." Moonshine winced. "Let me know when that's happening so I can get far away."

"Ass."

A few weeks later, Summerbird arrived. She bounded in with joy, wearing a dog shape Droplet hadn't seen before. Nearly fifteen years since Droplet's first visit to Panithen, nearly ten years since the colony became the place where she visited and not the place where she belonged...the colony must have found so many more people worthy of honor since she'd left.

My Droplet! said Summerbird. Her tail wagged furiously, nearly toppling a decorative table in the entryway. Droplet became a dog to greet her mother in kind, and for a few minutes, all was well.

They play-wrestled. They licked each other's faces. Summerbird shared news of the colony. Moss ambled in as a monitor lizard to join the greetings and conversation, though with less saliva and tail-wagging.

Then Summerbird asked, **Are you ready to come to the caravan?**

I'm not going, Droplet said in frantic movements, as if she could get this over with sooner if she moved fast enough.

Summerbird looked puzzled. **You're not?**

You never asked. You assumed I would, Droplet said. Her hackles rose with no conscious input.

But this...this is our purpose, Droplet. To know all there is to know. To learn what we can so we'll all become one and walk the stars again. And the sea! There's so much to know!

I know this is important, Mom. But what I'm doing here is important too.

Summerbird's face had gone sorrowful and confused, as if she couldn't understand what Droplet was saying. She whirled on Moss with a growl. **What have you been telling my child?**

Leave Moss out of this! Droplet said. **This is my choice. I'm doing good work here, Mom. I'm helping people.**

And what are you learning for *your* people? Summerbird said, with tiny, dainty movements that meant she was *really* upset.

What is the *point* of learning if we don't do something with our knowledge? I learned what's happening to people here. I can't leave them.

That's the whole point of what we do. To leave this world one day. You think any of this will matter when we're back among the stars?

It matters to the people who are still here, Droplet said.

My own child doesn't even know her name yet, and she's rejecting our own kind. Who will let you into the desert halls of the archive to claim your name, hm? Or are you going to stay

nameless for—

ENOUGH, Moss said, becoming a panther as she spoke. She growled at Summerbird, a growl that went beyond language to express a universal threat. **You will not speak to our child like that.**

Moss..., said Droplet.

Our child, hm? *Our* **child? She has clearly lost all respect for me, is that** *our* **doing?**

They were nose-to-nose now, their fur on end, growling fit to shake the room.

Droplet tried to wedge herself between them. **I made this choice! Me! And I can do it without my name, without anyone telling me to do it, because it's the right thing to do. So** *stop it.*

Her parents backed away from each other, still growling. Yelarcha burst in from the hallway, ready to fight, but she retreated slowly when she saw the entangled shapeshifters.

Summerbird turned away from Moss, toward Droplet. Moss stood beside Droplet, but Summerbird ignored her old friend altogether.

I don't know when I will next see you, if you do not come with us, she said. **If your own mother means anything to you, surely you will spend a day with me before I go. Then we can say proper farewells.**

That was exactly what I planned, Mother, Droplet said, annoyed. She didn't get to present this as a peace offering, now, nor a sign that she really was a good child. Now she looked reactive and petty. And her mother was still leaving. But she didn't have to face this alone. **Moss should join us as we talk. You two will not see each other for a long time either.**

Do you have any idea how long the ocean voyage will be? Moss asked. Her fur had lowered, and she licked a paw with a cat's typical feigned indifference.

Years upon years. The oceans are deep and wide, said Droplet's mother. **Perhaps after we travel, thanks to us, others will know**

how long such a voyage will take.

Moss flicked her gaze toward Droplet for a moment, then raised her eyes toward the ceiling, imploring the stars she could not see.

Then I will be honored to spend the day with you and our child before you leave.

Chapter Fourteen

After a quick stop in a room full of spare clothes, god tokens, bone wards, and other items one might use for a disguise—positioned conveniently near the secret back entrance—Droplet had clothes to fit her new form. This one was tall and olive-skinned, with close-cropped hair and tattoos of the Air Deity. None of the bone wards were as effective as the dragon one she'd dropped, but they'd have to do, and the church did have some turtle-shell fragments.

The back exit led into a lumber warehouse. With such a collection of dead tree matter, the Eyes couldn't see in. Droplet could hear distant voices, but she avoided them easily as she maneuvered around stacked wood until she was outside. She saw no Eyes on the walls around the warehouse. Good. By the time one picked her up, they wouldn't be able to pinpoint where she'd come from.

Crossing Hell Street to go south was much easier in the morning; most of the tourists were presumably sleeping in. Away from the crush of the promenade, morning in Sacarus was almost pleasant. The water lapped gently at the sides of the city. Shopkeepers unbarred their doors and neighbors called "hello" to each other. The smells of baking bread, spices, and window-box flowers filled the empty streets. In the relative cool of the early morning, they could almost mask the stench of sewage below, and occasionally on, the streets.

The Port Authority Records headquarters sparkled. A giant Eye watched from each side of the door, the black lines as thick as Droplet's arm. With the steps and the doorway between the Eyes, the building looked like a giant's face rising from beneath the stones of the city.

Droplet tried to look grumpy and unimpressed as she walked in without breaking stride. The grumpiness, at least, came naturally. The reception room rose two stories. Panels of brown, red, and white stone made a sunburst shape on the floor. On the ceiling and walls, some sycophantic artists had done frescoes depicting the glory of Sacarus. Or at least that's what she assumed they showed. She didn't know much about art.

Two receptionists, one human and one raptor, sat at a desk in front of a wall of keys. Based on their god-clips, both were devotees of the River Deity. The human looked up when Droplet walked in. "Name and purpose?" ne said.

Droplet channeled a smidgen of her frustration at being stuck on records duty *again*. "Ani of Portside—er, working for Gamielus. Hi. Look, I've only been here for a week. The island management hired me for the midsummer party, but we're missing thirty barrels of wine, and they sent me to track them down." Ani was a common name for an Air devotee, Portside the nearest major city. Gamielus held the biggest midsummer party of the private islands. Droplet treasured uninteresting cover stories: humans could be so inattentive when they were bored.

The receptionist turned and examined the keys behind ner, stretching ner hand into the air as ne thought, and some kind of air barrier rippled over the keys.

The receptionist led Droplet out of the lobby and farther into the building without making small talk. Droplet felt she had successfully walked the tightrope of mild unpleasantness—not angry enough that she'd stand out in the memory, but grumpy enough that sensible people would not try to chat, or pry, or stick around to find out more about this suspiciously generic human.

The low ceilings hemmed Droplet in, as did the aisles barely wide enough for a raptor to turn without their tail knocking into the shelves. Wooden grating protected the records themselves, but behind the stripes of wood, Droplet saw neat volumes lined up by date. Her heart leapt. A clearly marked filing system? Maybe the gods were smiling on her after all. Sure, aside from the dates, she understood few of the symbols on the spines and shelves, but she could learn. She could even ask the receptionist. What a concept!

She reminded herself that she was still, both in and out of character, very unhappy to be stuck on records duty. She scowled at some of the well-organized shelves in passing.

The receptionist led her to a large basement room where the filing shelves gave way to open tables and clusters of people. Raptors and humans flipped through loose papers, peered at waterlogged notebooks, and jotted down text in meticulous handwriting. On the ceiling, a few Eyes watched.

"Here's everything in the past month, minus some of yesterday. Some captains don't understand the value of prompt record keeping," ne said darkly, in a tone that suggested that these lax captains had been thoroughly punished for their failures. "Did your boss have a plan for where to look?" the receptionist continued, gesturing to the many, many filled shelves of the room.

"It should have shown up two days ago," said Droplet. She didn't know how long the blood mages had been assembling their captives, but they should have had almost all of them in place within the past couple days.

The receptionist led her to the appropriate cabinet and unlocked a pair of doors. "If you need anything else, see the floor supervisor," ne said, waving toward a harried raptor who was in the middle of what seemed to be an intense conversation about the size of decimal points. The receptionist strode off without waiting for an answer.

Droplet mentally patted herself on the back. One obstacle overcome.

She peered at the volume spines. Yes, truly a filing system of beauty—the handwriting was neat, and the scribes all seemed to agree on consistent spellings for the island names, even if the spellings didn't match Rangitam's map. Mother Enneth had knocked two more off the list of suspect islands, bringing the total down to nine. Gamielus wasn't on the list. Mother Enneth had heard stories of Gamielus parties spilling into the wine cellars and overtaking the attic; there'd be no place amidst the debauchery to hide a massive blood sacrifice. Droplet didn't want to pull down volumes for all nine islands at once, so she picked the three farthest from the main island and got to work.

Within the individual volumes, although the handwriting remained neat, the semblance of order began to break down. Shipments were entered in order of arrival. If there was any rhyme or reason to the indexing of the provided manifests, Droplet couldn't tell. Worse, the goods were labeled in shorthand. Some of the shorthand overlapped with what she'd seen in different cities—the abbreviations for "wheat" and "flour" were the same everywhere on the coast—but what was "iced blue"? A wine? A fruit? What could possibly be meant by "JFVL"? Record-deciphering had always been a puzzle of absence that, for some unknown reason, Moss enjoyed doing in her spare time—you had to make deductions based on what was missing.

Droplet reminded herself repeatedly that this was only temporary. She wouldn't be stuck on records duty forever, and surely this was better than facing the blood mages head-on. Maybe when she got back to Ninuthen, she could finally convince Moss that if Moss loved these kinds of puzzles so much, *she* could take records duty.

The hour bell chimed a couple times. She eliminated one of the three islands from her first set, and two of the three from her second set. Party supplies and "feeding cult hostages" supplies were bound to be different, but some overlapped. Especially if one was hosting a really bad party.

She was starting in on volume seven when she tried to stretch her back and realized she couldn't move anything below her ribs. She tried to make a sound, and nothing came out.

A feathery hand patted her shoulder.

"Let's you and I have a chat, shall we?" said a familiar raptor voice. "I'm going to lift this spell from your legs for a moment, and you are not going to try anything brave or daring or foolish." Her voice made it clear that as far as she was concerned, those were all synonyms.

Droplet's head and heart raced. What had she done wrong? How had the blood mages figured it out? She turned her head to glare, masking the fear. She recognized Isna, the raptor who had led the blood mages at the inn.

Isna smiled at her, all teeth.

Droplet followed Isna through the maze of bookshelves, going in a different direction than how she'd entered. She searched for any avenue of escape, but Eyes watched from every angle. Droplet was not so naïve that she thought the Eyes, or whoever looked out through them, would be any help. Her turtle-shell bone had done nothing against the blood mage, and no matter what shape she took, the blood mage could react.

Isna led them into a small, neat office, with its own personal shelves full of impeccably aligned ledgers. "Sit," Isna said, gesturing at the one spare chair while sealing some kind of ward over the door. The bare, cream-colored walls didn't have a single Eye on them.

"You do realize that shapeshifters aren't *common*," the raptor said.

Droplet didn't say anything, just glared as Isna circled around and took the chair behind the massive oak desk. Was this her own office, or had she commandeered someone else's to look more impressive?

When Droplet didn't say anything, Isna continued, "When

Sacarus gets report of a dangerous fugitive shapeshifter, they don't simply forget about it overnight. Every single new tourist is under suspicion. Now there are a *lot* of tourists, grant you, and a *lot* of temporary labor. The Eyes have at least a dozen false leads running on you, I'd wager. But the Eyes aren't part of my flock, and my flock and I know who you're looking for. I can't tell you how pleased I am that you sat in my building for hours while we looked into that paper-thin alibi."

"*Your* building?" Droplet said.

"I don't own it, but I work here. Contrary to what some devotees might have led you to believe, most of the faithful do have jobs like anyone else," Isna said with a twist of her mouth.

At least if Droplet was going to die, she would die at the hands of someone who also held obvious contempt for Solvim. Small pleasures.

She felt like her hands were shaking, but when she glanced down, they sat still in her lap.

"You thought I would let you shapeshift? Please," said the raptor. Hope sprang in Droplet's heart—Isna didn't know what she'd been doing! She *wasn't* reading her thoughts! Never before had sitting back and letting the other person monologue worked so well for Droplet.

"So what happens now?" Droplet said.

"First, you're going to answer my questions about this hare-brained 'rescue mission' you're on. Next, you're going to stop interfering."

"Yeah, that's likely," Droplet said. Her voice didn't waver. But Isna gave her a look full of pity. Gods, she hated that look.

"Where is your necromantic companion?"

"The Church of the Constant Flame," Droplet said, and hissed in shock. "What did you do?!"

The raptor held up her left arm. On the dark feathers, Droplet could see the telltale trickle of blood. Droplet flinched. "I didn't think a shapeshifter would be squeamish," Isna said, resting her arms on the desk so Droplet could still see the glisten of light reflecting off the blood. No, the blood *itself* was shining. Droplet tried to focus on that and not the implications of the raptor's words. She knew something about shapeshifters. Droplet wasn't about to ask her exactly how much she knew.

"What did you do to me?" she growled.

"I made some suggestions." She took out paper and pen. Droplet tried to look inside her own mind—how could she do that? There had to be some way around this spell, something in her head that would seem *off* that she could cast out. "Now, the necromancer's name..."

"Azera Carpenter."

"Really? You weren't working with a fake name? Is this your first time at this?"

"No," Droplet hissed through gritted teeth. The raptor laughed. Droplet wanted to lunge at her. She wanted to be a bear, a lion, something with claws and real teeth. But she couldn't change.

"Did you figure out where Harra is in those couple hours?"

"No," Droplet said. She'd never felt so helpless.

"Good. Though if your necromancer is working with those pesky nuns, we should do something about that."

Someone knocked on the door, three long taps followed by three short.

"Come in," said Isna. A lanky human with an Air tattoo entered—vaguely familiar. Droplet may have seen ver at the records tables.

"Ma'am, do you still need me to disguise the records?"

"No need. Thank you, Merrite. Garshal would kill me if I tampered with the records for anything less than certain discovery. He's our treasurer this year," she added to Droplet, as if Droplet was a guest and this was a perfectly normal conversation to be having in one's place of employment.

"You have a rotating treasurer? Are you serious?" Droplet said. Isna fixed her with a disapproving scowl. "We have for decades."

"Nobody appreciates how much earthly coordination it takes to keep the guardians alive," said Merrite piously.

"The rotation is so nobody gets too greedy," Isna continued.

"Gosh, corruption? In a cult that kidnaps people for blood sacrifice? I am *astonished*, I tell you."

Isna sighed and massaged her temple with her feathery claws. "I see you won't be open to some friendly conversation."

"When did you figure that one out?"

"You strolled into my building and sat for hours, so you're in no position to talk about powers of observation," snapped the raptor.

"It's only fair that we try to bring even the most stubborn souls to the light," said Merrite. Ve seemed to be chiding Droplet, as if Droplet was the one at fault for not being effectively converted.

And if you don't convert me? Droplet thought, but she didn't let herself ask. She would find out the answer sooner than she liked anyway.

Her fear must have shown on her face despite her best efforts, because Isna's face suddenly changed. Droplet thought the leader of the cultists was trying to look kind.

"You have us all wrong, you know. What would you do, to keep the world safe? And our honored guests—"

Droplet laughed.

"Our *honored guests* are certainly better off here than in whatever hovels we dragged them from. We give them every luxury. What else would you do, for people who keep the world safe? We're not monsters."

"Of course you aren't. You're deluded, self-righteous sadists. Give me an honest monster any day."

The attempt at kindness on Isna's face vanished, leaving her colder and crueler than before. "Your necromancer may be more receptive once we've caught up to her. Believe what you want. Your opinion no longer matters."

"Isna!" said Merrite.

"Guardians' sake, Merrite, I'm not going to kill her, were you not listening? No, she's going to shift into a rat for us."

Droplet had shifted into a rat uncountable times throughout her life. She liked rats, the clever little things.

She'd never been forced to shift before.

Her body squished and squeezed in on itself without any input from her. Her hands shriveled into paws as she collapsed into the borrowed clothing. She felt every grind and crush of shifting matter for a long, agonizing moment. And then she was a rat, and wondered, *What does this accomplish?*

With the rat's eyesight, she could barely make out the folds of the clothes around her. The world was full of new smells, though. Rats had been here, in this room, though not since the previous night. The smell of human and raptor stood out clearly now, as did the odor of books. Most intriguingly to the new nose, Isna kept some jerky, crackers, and a myriad of other snacks in her desk.

She still couldn't move her legs.

She twitched her tail experimentally. That could move.

Suddenly, light and a rush of air. Someone must have pulled the clothes away. And still Droplet couldn't move. She stood stuck between two blurry, lumbering towers. No, not entirely stuck. Her head and torso and whiskers and nose and ears were trembling.

"Now what?" said Merrite.

"I hear the rats of this city do very well for themselves. She's going to think she's a rat."

What? That doesn't make any sense. You can't just...do that...

She felt a gentle shove, like a pillow falling on her.

The world unraveled.

She was exposed. She was out in the open with enemies watching—how had she gotten here? How could she have been so stupid? Was it a dream? Surely it was a dream, trapped and frozen while predators closed in—

No. She could move.

She shot away from the light, following the familiar scent of other rats. She couldn't figure out quite what they meant, and that frustrated her. She must have eaten something poisoned. This happened all the time to rats...to other rats. She shook her head as she ran, hoping to clear it.

She heard a reproving voice behind her. "So she's completely a rat now?"

"Are you questioning my spellwork, Merrite?" said the other voice from on high.

"N-no. Of course not. Forgive me."

"And besides, this was the best way to..."

But Droplet wasn't listening. The big ones could argue. Kept them distracted. She'd spotted a way out.

Behind a giant boxy thing—a shelf, some part of her brain supplied—near the corner, her kind had gnawed a hole in the wall. She understood completely. The room held a treasure of snacks—that must be why she was here, out in the open. She'd gotten careless. Taken too many risks.

She didn't recognize the rat smells, but that didn't bother her. Rats would protect their own. They would help her.

She bolted into the tunnel and breathed a sigh of relief as the walls closed in.

Safe.

Chapter Fifteen

With the immediate threat gone, Droplet reassessed the shreds of her mind. To state the obvious, something had gone terribly wrong. How had she gotten into that room? Unclear. She was a long way from home, she knew. Who was her family? She could remember scents, but faintly, as if they'd walked there weeks before, and the bits she remembered made no sense, all jumbled up with other animals, including a host of predators.

She needed to help someone, warn someone, but whenever she tried to figure out who, she saw a human, but in a way she couldn't have possibly seen with her eyes—in sharp focus, and in colors these eyes couldn't see, and *small*. She saw a half-cat too, which was of course out of the question. But even with that dismissed— the half-cat was a fleeting image, dark and running, easy to place as a trick of her fractured mind—the human remained. How could she be helping a human? Did it have something to do with the human and raptor that had seen her and let her go?

She felt alone, but that was a familiar feeling, and she held onto it. She'd been lonely for a long time before. The specifics were lost, but the feeling was as sharp as a bite. That was real.

By the time Droplet found another rat, she was feeling *extremely* sorry for herself. She nearly ran over them as she rounded a corner.

The rat squeaked, scrabbling backward.

"Sorry, sorry!" said Droplet, by rubbing her whiskers. "I'm lost and confused," she added, by scent and squeak and motion. She knew, as she spoke, that she was out of practice with this and hadn't communicated with her full body in a while. What had she been *doing*?

The new rat sniffed her from nose to rump, and she sniffed him back. He was healthy, he'd been eating well, he'd spent a lot of time in the sewers, and he came from a large colony. He was very polite about his own introductory sniffs, but when he finished, he was as confused as she was.

"Who are you?" he asked.

"Droplet, but I don't know anything else," she said. "I think I was poisoned."

"You were cursed," he said. "I smell the secret snack room on you. That raptor is *mean*. Lots of family get tripped up in there. Did you get snacks?"

"No," Droplet said, sadly, and he licked her face to cheer her up. She licked him back, hoping that was the polite thing to do. Bits and pieces of memory floated back to her, but not enough to be useful. Rats had their own customs, and as a stranger here, she'd have to follow their lead and learn. She hadn't been to this colony before.

Why was she thinking "rats" like a word said from the outside?

"We have food to share here while you're confused! The magic goes away after a while. I am Cheesebreath!"

"A lucky name," Droplet complimented him. "As I said, I am Droplet."

"An...inventive name," he said in return after a brief hesitation. "Come, come!"

She followed Cheesebreath. They scurried for only a few min-utes until the unmistakable scents of a thriving rat colony reached her nose. Squeaks and drips of water from up ahead echoed in a way that meant "space," but she was still awed when they left the winding tunnel and emerged into a...*catacomb*, said that odd part of her brain. They entered at the ceiling of an underground room so spacious that her whiskers and ears couldn't detect the far end.

Forgotten, faded lightstones shed what little light there was, and even they were nearly covered with fungus and moss. The rubble they scuttled down must have once held fine mosaics, judging by the regular changes in texture under her feet, smooth-rough, smooth-rough.

Debris piles emerged from the flooded catacomb's depths to form a dry-ish surface that rats could cross. And there were many, many rats. Droplet relaxed a fraction as she followed Cheesebreath past each contented scene—nests of babies nursing at their mothers, young rats chasing each other's tails on the flotsam below, older rats grooming each other and reminiscing about meals they'd plundered in seasons past. A peaceful home. In some ways familiar, but in others, not. Things would be so much easier if only she could remember which was which...

Cheesebreath introduced her to a whirlwind of colony members. Droplet did her best to connect names with scents, but Cheesebreath assured her it was fine if she misremembered. The rats in the colony were all familiar with curses.

"You'll be ready to tackle any trash heap in a few days," said one heavily scarred rat, clearly speaking from her personal experience.

"I don't think I have a few days," Droplet said, worried. "There's something I've forgotten, but I know it was urgent." The rat nuzzled her. Droplet nuzzled back. She was tempted to stay still and let the community welcome her. Some nice mutual grooming, maybe sleeping in a pile. Even with her mind in pieces, she knew she had been missing that for a very long time. But that was a temptation she couldn't give into, not now, not ever. For...reasons. Yes, she was sure she had very good reasons hidden somewhere in her lost memories.

Nobody in the colony recognized her.

Cheesebreath moved fast, his eagerness never wavering. Soon, they'd talked to everyone but the elders. Droplet didn't remember how her colony had been run, but the way Cheesebreath said "the elders" left no doubt as to who ran this one.

They clambered up to a hollow in the wall where two stones had fallen out. A group of old rats sat content in their nests, much like the other clusters of old ones she'd met around the catacomb. One of the rats here was regaling the others with a tale of a crow she'd fought for a chicken dumpling. As she saw the new arrivals, she broke off and scurried to meet them with glee. She had three legs and one-and-a-half ears, and even among a colony of happy rats, she stood out for her smell of health and good eating.

"Cheesebreath! And a guest, I see. Which colony are you from? Dockside? Bridgeside?" she asked.

"I...I don't know," Droplet said.

"He's cursed, ma'am," said Cheesebreath.

He? No, that's not right, is it? Droplet thought. But of the many mysteries facing her, that one was a low priority, and she refrained from correcting her guide.

"Droplet, this is Beef Stew," Cheesebreath continued.

"I'm honored, ma'am," Droplet said.

"Don't be," said Beef Stew cheerfully. "Curses! Nasty things. You'd best lay up with us for a few days."

"I don't think I can do that. I keep remembering I have to help someone." She didn't say *a human.*

"You'll be of no help to anyone during the sun-turn party," said Beef Stew.

"The what?"

"The big folk have the sun-turn party coming up tomorrow. Chaos! The streets will be packed, and the humans and raptors will be drunk—bad news for any rat who's caught out in it. Wait for *our* feast the next day, when the trash is still good and the big folk are miserable in their beds. Best eating all year, after the sun-turn."

"The sun-turn!" Droplet said. "No, no no no. I'm sorry, I can't wait. Something bad is happening on the sun-turn." She spun in a circle and paced back and forth in the narrow opening before the nest. Cheesebreath chittered in alarm, but Beef Stew and the other old rats settled in. "The raptor—the one who curses people—she's going after the person I'm helping. I had to help her do something before the sun-turn."

"Who are you helping? What did she smell like? Maybe we can help," Beef Stew said. Droplet dipped her nose to the ground and started grooming her whiskers, trying to think of a way to avoid this.

"My memory isn't good right now, and everything's very confused. But I think the person I had to help is a human."

Stunned stillness. Nobody twitched a whisker or even breathed. Beef Stew broke it. "A *human*?"

"It must be something about the curse," said Cheesebreath. His exuberance had snuffed out like a candle.

"In all ten of my seasons, I can't remember any curses that conjured imaginary humans," said Beef Stew.

"And I've heard nothing in the old stories about curses creating memories of humans, nothing at all," another elder, blind and mostly bald, said.

Droplet froze. They would know. They would know she didn't fit, that she didn't belong. She was deep in their home, and they would turn on her; she wouldn't be able to get out—

Cheesebreath licked her. She shivered, startling them both.

"You poor child," Beef Stew said, joining in the grooming.

"If we rule out the curse...perhaps this is not the curse, but something left behind. You hear stories of rats being friendly with humans and raptors and suchlike," said an elder missing an ear.

Cheesebreath gasped.

"It seems Cheesebreath has not been listening to the stories much," Beef Stew teased.

"Of course not. He's one of Mushgrab's boys, isn't he? That family can never keep still," said the ear-missing elder, approval clear in her body language.

"Never understood those who truck with big folk myself, but it takes all sorts of rats for a colony," said Beef Stew. "So long as nobody goes leading any of them here," she added.

"Never!" said Droplet, outraged. Lead *humans* to a rat's home? Unthinkable! Really, the whole colony seemed much more open toward humans than she was. The untrustworthy, deceptive species that could tear your world up...

...and yet...

She could remember that one human, someone new in her life. She liked that human. She had even considered trusting that human.

Most of her life was lost to fog, but she knew like she knew her own paw that the human was in danger, and she, Droplet, was responsible for keeping her safe.

She'd lost the thread of rat conversation. The elders seemed to be sharing stories of rats who had grown fond of the big folk and met bad ends. Droplet could almost tell the stories herself—only the details were different. You think this one will care for you, and then other humans come along...

Another face! She could remember the face of a human that had betrayed her before. See? Why would Azera be any different?

Azera. A name! That was new!

Maybe all her memories would come back before the sun-turn, but Droplet didn't want to bet on it.

"You are of course welcome to stay here as long as you wish. We'll check in with the other colonies after the sun-turn, if you're still cursed, and see if we can help you find where you're from," said Beef Stew.

"You'll always have a home with us, if you want!" said the one-eared elder. "Always room for a nice-smelling young man in this colony."

"But we can't do anything until after the sun-turn, you understand. It wouldn't be safe for you or any of us," Beef Stew continued.

Cheesebreath nuzzled her again. "I can take you to the scrap pile, if you'd like. There's plenty of soft nests with room for a new friend."

She was tempted. Stars, she was tempted. Droplet couldn't remember the last time she'd felt safe, and she got the feeling that once the curse lifted, even the vague sense of safety she felt in the colony would be gone again.

She remembered talking with the human—Azera.

"I'm going to be looking out for you anyway, whether you like it or not."

I'm ridiculous, thought Droplet. But she knew the right thing to do. This Azera was in trouble. She planted her paws firmly on the stone and took a deep breath. "I'm very grateful for your hospitality. But once I've had some food and a brief rest, I'll have to go. I can't rest while someone is counting on me. Even a human."

Beef Stew and a couple of the elders nodded approvingly, while the one-eared elder sighed.

"We never keep the nice-smelling ones around," she complained.

Droplet ate heartily. The rats had stocked up before the sunturn and were happy to share. When she prepared to say her goodbyes to Cheesebreath, though, he said, "I'm coming with you."

"No," she said. She had the strangest sense that this had all happened before.

"You're cursed. You need help," said Cheesebreath. Droplet bristled, mostly because he was right. She *was* cursed. She had no idea which way to go out of the colony, how to get back to Azera.

"It's not safe. Won't your elders be mad?" she tried.

"Oh, they'll just chitter and go 'One of Mushgrab's, all right,' but with their whiskers set so you can tell they're really very proud of you even though they're scolding," said Cheesebreath.

Droplet's nose twitched in delight. "Is Mushgrab here?"

"No, Mom died fighting a cat so five of the colony could get away. We've got songs about her! I can sing them to you if you'd like."

Droplet didn't have the heart to say no, but she also didn't have the fortitude to say yes. Instead, she said, "You know you don't have to help a rat you just met."

"You're trying to help a *human* while you're *cursed*. I think between the two of us, I'm the more sensible one," he said in perfect seriousness. "So! Where are we going?"

Droplet thought about it. Where had she left the human? She let her mind drift back. She could see a building...it looked too small relative to her size. Maybe what she recalled was a picture of the building? She tried to remember the smells, but they were muffled, like she'd scented them through a mattress. The sounds... There had been lots of big people there. And the building kept out magic. That had been important.

"A building with lots of people and no magic. Good food." She conveyed the smells as best as she could.

Cheesebreath nodded. "I think I know where you mean! There's only one place on the island without magic, and their trash pile is the *best*. I'm so happy I'm going with you—the others will be so jealous!"

"Even on the sun-turn?"

"Even on the sun-turn."

The maze of Sacarus was confusing enough for the big folk (*How do I know that?* Droplet wondered). It was magnitudes worse for rats.

Cheesebreath led Droplet along what he assured her was the best way. They scrabbled through ancient, dark pipes, clambered up and down through grates in the street, scuttled around corners of buildings and through the shelter of trash heaps. Even with a full belly, the temptation to stop and snack was high. So many delicious smells!

But of course, crumbling bricks, puddles of dirty water, and tight crevasses were the easy part. In a city, most every creature bigger than a rat wanted to kill rats.

Cheesebreath narrated the hazards to Droplet as they went. This alley was home to a tomcat—stay beneath the trash heap. A falcon nested over this square, so if they got separated, stick to cover. The bakery smelled good, but there was poison in every corner. He kept a cheery tone as he talked, but she could see the tension in his nose and whiskers. Droplet wanted to bolt or fight. Both of those reactions would most likely get her dead. Unless she fought something very small, but that wouldn't be satisfying.

The worst part of the journey, though, came near the end.

They had to cross Hell Street.

They didn't have to cross *over* the street, thank goodness, but only a few open pipes ran under it. "You're lucky it's a dry day, or there would be no way through!" said Cheesebreath.

Every rat knew these highways. So too did everything that fed on rats.

They started their journey around midafternoon. By the tilt of the shadows, the trip to the pipe entrance had taken only an hour. Maybe the way time had stretched into endless terror, taut muscles, and twitching whiskers was part of the curse, but Droplet suspected it wasn't. She'd done this sort of risky thing before, many times. She couldn't remember when. But it always felt like this.

The pipe Cheesebreath had chosen was short and narrow, only wide enough for a single rat. Cheesebreath tried to lead the way, but Droplet stopped him.

"What do you think you're doing?" she asked.

"I have to go first," he said.

"This pipe goes straight under the street, right?" she said.

"Yes."

"No turns or drops?"

"No, it's a good pipe."

"Then let me go first."

"But the one who goes first will get caught!"

"Yes, and it can't be you! You're a nice young rat with a colony full of people who love you."

"You must have a colony too, you just don't remember them," Cheesebreath said earnestly.

Droplet thought about it. She remembered...Moss! Moss was important, for sure. She could even remember a flash of Moss as a burly rat, guiding her along the cobblestones of some street far from here. But was that it?

She tried to conjure up some scent or sound of her mother but found only bitter, resentful loss. The same sort of loss she'd felt every time today she'd tried to remember her own colony.

"I think almost everyone's gone," she said to Cheesebreath. She wanted to lie down on the ground right there. "One of my parents is far away, my mother is gone, and I can't remember any brothers or sisters or aunts or uncles or family or friends. There's only this human."

Cheesebreath nuzzled her and leaned against her. Droplet leaned against him in return. They stayed that way until they noticed a distant cat watching them from behind a flowerpot.

Without waiting for Cheesebreath's input, Droplet bolted into the pipe.

"Droplet!" Cheesebreath ran behind her, squeaking.

No rats or mice were attempting to come the other way, though many crickets hopped out of Droplet's path. Roaches scurried up the sides of the walls. Droplet paid them no mind. The whole pipe thrummed with the reverberation of dozens of feet on the street overhead.

When she reached the other end of the pipe, she stopped. She sniffed. She listened. And here she discovered one particular obstacle that Cheesebreath hadn't mentioned. This opening was right next to the street, and the sounds and smells of the stampede of big folk completely drowned out other sensory cues. It was impossible to detect any useful information. She smelled roasting dumplings and heard booming voices talking of the weather, the plans for their party, the unique vases on sale for the discerning customer...

An entire pride of lions could have been watching the tunnel, and she wouldn't know a thing.

Her murky eyes could make out empty space in front of her, wide enough for a couple humans. The blocky shape of the shadows suggested bins of trash or boxes tossed aside.

Cheesebreath, behind her, said, "There's places to hide in the alley straight ahead. Once we get there it's much safer."

Droplet acknowledged his advice with a twitch of her tail.

The outside world wasn't getting any clearer.

She bolted.

The murky space around the exit was not hiding a pride of lions. It was, though, hiding a thin, mangy terrier who pounced the instant her body was free.

Droplet squealed. She squirmed and lashed, trying to bite or claw, but the terrier's paws held her firm.

"Let me go!"

"Let him go!" Cheesebreath squeaked from the tunnel. He bounded out to snarl and bounded back in again. The terrier sniffed at her, and Droplet could see up close those jaws that would lock on and shake her and snap her neck.

"Please! I have a human!" she said.

The terrier stopped and cocked her head. "You have...a human?" she said.

"She's in trouble, and I have to get back to her," Droplet babbled.

Keeping Droplet firmly pinned, the dog sat on her haunches. "I didn't think rats could have humans," she said.

"We can so have humans," Cheesebreath said with all the

indignation of someone defending a fact he had learned earlier that morning. The terrier barked at him, but he didn't back away.

"How are *you* going to help a human?" said the terrier.

"How does a dog help a human?" Droplet said. She tried to hold back her scorn, mindful of the paws pinning her. "I'm small, but size isn't important, is it? What's important is being there for her."

She believed this was true with all her furiously beating heart. She couldn't let herself doubt. The question of how, exactly, she was going to help the human Azera was one she hadn't let herself confront head-on. Sometimes things were important even if you didn't know why. She was pretty sure that was true even when she wasn't cursed.

The terrier's eyes got all wobbly, like dogs' do. Droplet continued, "Did you ever have a human?"

"I did," said the dog.

"Then you know we have to help humans, right? Especially the silly ones. They can barely smell! She needs me," Droplet pleaded.

The dog's eyes became even more soulful. How could they do that? It wasn't fair. With great solemnity, the terrier let Droplet up.

Cheesebreath was ready to bolt, but Droplet merely stood up and gave herself a shake.

"Thank you," she said.

"You need help!" the terrier said.

"Er..."

"You are in danger. I will guard you," said the terrier. Droplet considered this offer. Everyone knew it was the small dogs you had to watch out for. But everyone also knew dogs couldn't lie to save their souls.

(Who was "everyone"? Droplet couldn't remember any other rats saying that...)

"We would be honored," said Droplet. She motioned for Cheesebreath to join her, and he did, trembling. She described the building they were going for, and the terrier's stubby tail wagged furiously.

"The nuns are the best humans! Your human must be a good one."

Nuns? Is Azera a nun? Droplet wondered. She was almost positive Azera was not a nun, and for some reason she was relieved to remember this.

With the terrier leading them, the journey became much easier. The terrier kept away from Hell Street and growled at anyone, whether raptor or human, cat or dog, who took an unfriendly interest in Droplet and Cheesebreath. When big folk smiled or laughed at the sight, on the other hand, the terrier held her head higher, tail wagging. Perhaps she could parlay this into some treats—maybe even a new human.

They reached the building without further incident. The doors went up and up, far beyond what Droplet could see. She stared until Cheesebreath nudged her.

"What are you looking at? This isn't the kitchen!"

Right, the kitchen door. Why would she use the front door?

They traveled around the building into a small, weedy courtyard with a deliciously pungent heap of rotting scraps. At the kitchen door, the terrier pawed and whined. Droplet fought the instinctive urge to flee at the sound of scrabbling, stubby dog claws. Cheesebreath trembled; she leaned against him to offer him comfort.

The door opened and they both jumped, but they didn't run.

"Hey girl! Let me see if I have something—" The towering human spotted Cheesebreath and Droplet. "Out! Shoo! Get—"

The terrier jumped in front of Cheesebreath and Droplet, shielding them with her body. The human froze in the doorway. The terrier barked again and wagged her tail.

The human sighed, a long-suffering sound.

"Sister Caresil, can you ask Mother Enneth if any of our guests is expecting a stray dog and two rats?"

"Rats?!" a distant voice echoed.

"It's not any stranger than the ghost pigeon that one time."

"Less hygienic, though," the second voice said.

Droplet squeaked in indignation.

"What are they saying? Do you know?" Cheesebreath asked.

Droplet relayed the conversation as human feet stomped into the distance. The terrier sat on her haunches to wait.

Light, cautious human footsteps approached, along with the tapping of a stick. A papery voice said, "Huh. Really, two rats and a dog. My word."

"Did you not believe Sister Caresil?" said the first voice with a touch of impatience.

"Oh, I believed you saw these all right, but I thought surely this would be some kind of trick or illusion. But the wards seem to be in proper working condition."

"Mother, with all due respect..."

"Yes, yes, child, I'll go ask our guests."

Time dripped by. The sister who had discovered them took pity on them and tossed out a leftover sausage. The terrier even offered to share a few nibbles with them. Droplet declined; she would feel wrong taking food from the strangers who had helped her. Cheesebreath ate with gusto.

"Once my human arrives, can you take Cheesebreath home safely?" Droplet asked the terrier. Cheesebreath looked alarmed, but the terrier agreed in an instant.

"I...I can get there myself, it will be okay..." said Cheesebreath.

"Nonsense! You are honorable, rat. Why, any dog would be proud to—"

Droplet stopped paying attention to their conversation because she heard more footsteps approaching: shod human feet and bare paws. She recognized the tread. She started forward up the stairs, stopping only at the first sister's "NO."

"Ah, sister, we thought these might be for us? We weren't expecting so many..."

Rangitam. The voice had a name! A face! A dog-human, and

though that combination of species should have sparked fear on multiple levels, Droplet knew with deep certainty that this was a friend.

She squeaked.

The two new shapes appeared in the narrow doorway; the sister stepped back. She still couldn't see their faces well, but she knew the smells.

"Is...is one of you Droplet?" said Azera.

Droplet squeaked and bounced, all words forgotten.

"Droplet! What the hells is going on?" Azera said.

"She made friends," Rangitam said as if this was the most adorable thing he had ever laid eyes on.

"Right, right. Can you understand her like this?"

"My grasp of the shapeshifter language is rusty—let's bring her in."

"You are not walking a *rat* through our kitchen!" said the sister.

"She's not a rat," Rangitam said patiently.

What? Droplet thought. Then Azera leaned down and scooped her up in her hands.

Oh. She felt like she'd plunged into ice melt in the mountains. She shivered all over, shivered down to her bone marrow, as she felt the latent aura of necromancy wash the curse from her. Her broken and jumbled thoughts reconnected, the bits from the curse jamming into reality like recalcitrant puzzle pieces being forced into place.

Azera.

The blood mages.

The midsummer sacrifice.

The mages were coming for them.

That's why she'd had to race across the city.

First, payment where payment was due. "Thank you both," she said to Cheesebreath and the terrier. "I never would have made it without you. I'll see if I can get you some extra sausage before you go. I hope we'll meet again. Don't be scared."

"Scared by what?" Cheesebreath said, while the terrier wagged her tail.

Droplet turned into a myna bird.

Cheesebreath bolted under the terrier, who started barking up a storm. Well, at least now they seemed to be working together. Droplet turned to Rangitam and Azera—and, oh, right, the sister. Oh well. Their secret wouldn't have lasted long anyway.

The sister looked surprised, but only for a moment. Droplet supposed this was *less* wild than rats and terriers becoming allies. Using the humans' language, she said, "Sister, could you get those two more food? They didn't have to help me, but they did."

"Certainly. Are they...uh, are they...?"

"They're a normal rat and a normal dog," said Droplet. To Cheesebreath and the dog she tried to gesture, "Food's coming! Thanks again!" She didn't know if the birdlike gestures would work, but she hoped they would.

"Let's get inside," Rangitam said, surveying the walls. Droplet hadn't even thought to look for Eyes—but now that she did, she saw none. It seemed the Eyes were busy elsewhere. Rangitam closed the door behind them as they started through the kitchen.

"Droplet," said Azera. Reluctantly, Droplet looked Azera in the face. "What happened?"

What could she say? *I thought I was a rat, but now I'm better? I crossed the city convinced you were in mortal danger, and I'm almost glad I'm right because I would have felt pretty silly otherwise? I lost almost everything of who I was, and you were still there?*

She settled on, "The cultists got me—turns out the head one works in records. They know you're here now, so we have to run."

"How'd you escape?" asked Rangitam.

"She...she made me think I was a rat, then let me go."

"And you still found your way back here?" said Azera.

"Rats are very smart. I told you," said Droplet. She did *not* want to go into any more detail.

Gods, she was shaking again.

"How much do the cultists know?" asked Rangitam.

"They know Azera is here. They know Azera isn't a fake name. They know we're narrowing down the islands... I think that's all. They didn't mention anything about you," Droplet said. She focused on the facts and quashed the guilt. She had been under a spell. She couldn't have kept silent.

"And they're on their way?" Azera said.

"If they aren't here already. Is there anywhere else we can go?" Droplet asked Rangitam. He and Azera exchanged a glance and nodded at each other.

"Unless you narrowed down which island we're going to..." Azera said.

Droplet shook her head.

"Then we're going to the cemetery island," said Azera. "The living weren't much help."

Chapter Sixteen

Droplet and Azera took the same back exit through the lumberyard. Droplet used the most intimidating dog form she had, more wolf than dog, her shoulder higher than Azera's waist and mouth sporting a killer's snarl. This was from a dog named Mr. Sunshine, who'd been so flattered by Droplet's request to honor him by taking his form that he'd licked her whole head. But nobody needed to know that.

Rangitam would stay behind and hole up at the church until the solstice had passed or until he'd heard from them—whichever came first. He had no way to stand up to blood mages. He had hugged Droplet farewell after her transformation from bird to dog; she'd done her best to hug him back.

As they walked, Azera filled Droplet in on what she'd missed. Even with Mother Enneth's help, those at the church had only managed to eliminate one of the nine suspect islands during Droplet's adventure, and that was one of the ones Droplet had ruled out herself. They still had six islands left to search. And Azera had told Rangitam and Mother Enneth about her necromancy because she felt she had to be honest about her abilities if they were going to make real progress. Rangitam and Mother Enneth had both taken it well, she said, though Droplet suspected Azera had a very low bar for "well." At any rate, the two of them had helped devise this latest plan.

Azera had politely explained that she couldn't just ask the ether for a ghost who knew the cult's location. Even if such a ghost existed—debatable, given the memory-stealing nature of the cult—finding such a ghost would have been as hard as finding the cult in the living world. Instead, in this new plan, they needed as many ghosts as they could get.

Therefore, they needed a boat to take to the cemetery island. The Eyes monitored all the official ferries, so Droplet led them to the North Docks, full of people with personal boats looking to make a quick buck. Many of them had ties to some corrupt organization or another, be it a noble house or undercover Eyes or organized crime. None of those seemed the least bit threatening anymore. It had been a very, very long day. A whole eternity had passed in two days.

Mercifully, with Droplet in a dog's shape, she and Azera couldn't have a discussion. Droplet didn't know what to say. Occasionally, Azera would rest her hand on Droplet's head and lightly scratch. Her tail turned traitor and started wagging, but she could smell Azera calming in return, so she didn't object. That was of course the only reason she didn't object. It wasn't because petting made her want to roll on her back and beg for belly rubs. Definitely not.

Instead of talking to Azera or begging for belly rubs, Droplet struck terror into the hearts of innocent boat owners.

"We need a boat to the cemetery. Yes, we'll pay. No, I don't want to talk about why. Please respect my privacy as I grieve," Azera said, over and over.

Droplet growled at key moments. Mr. Sunshine's wolf ancestry had given her a baritone growl that seemed to reverberate off the surrounding stone. Humans and raptors alike fell over themselves to recommend high-quality boats that, crucially, were not their own boat.

"Maybe we're going about this wrong," Azera muttered after the fourth rejection. The sun was sinking, though sunset of course would be coming late. Shops were closing, boat captains tying off, and everywhere, they caught chatter about the midsummer festivities. "Can we try being polite? I'm so good at being nice." Droplet leaned against her and whuffed. For the next boat owner, she was the model of dog propriety. She sat on her haunches at a respectful distance, perked her ears, and let her tongue loll out of her mouth. Azera worked her magic. Droplet could only admire her acting.

The human who captained this little boat—bright green, getting on in years but perfectly sturdy—offered to take them for a reasonable-sounding price. Azera talked him down to one even more reasonable. All three of them fit in the boat, with about a foot of personal space each to spare. The human hummed as he rowed.

The breeze blew in from the ocean, and soon, the stink of city life was gone, replaced by a whole symphony of maritime odors that Droplet didn't recognize but her dog nose wished to explore more. Gulls cawed overhead. The experience could have been serene, except halfway across the channel, the human pulled a wand out and pointed it at Azera's chest, demanding all her money.

Azera laughed and laughed.

"You think this is a joke?" the human said.

"Gods, yes. Just row us the rest of the way, and we'll forget this ever happened, all right?"

Droplet started growling again. Either that growl or Azera's manic smile convinced him, because he picked up the oars and started rowing much faster.

The cemetery officially stayed open until sundown. The jumbled, mismatched array of tombs cast long shadows across the island. Azera and Droplet headed for the mausoleum where the less-fortunate were kept in the walls, every resting place barely large enough for a jar of cremated remains. The mausoleum sprawled on the island like a squashed spider, a mishmash of wings and extensions added over the centuries as the dead steadily accumulated.

Nobody was there.

Azera's grandmother helped them confirm the emptiness of the building.

Droplet and Azera had no idea whether this emptiness was normal for Sacarian cemeteries. Maybe Sacarians didn't like their dead much?

Droplet turned back into the human form she'd used at the nunnery and got dressed, then she and Azera sat down on the marble floor of one of the endless mausoleum rooms.

Azera placed her hands together. She shut her eyes for only a moment. When she opened them again, they sparkled with the reflected light of the plane of the dead.

A chill crawled over Droplet's skin. Azera's lips moved, but no sound came out—none that could be heard in the living world, anyway. After several minutes, ghosts appeared, slow and then in a rush, like a rainstorm. A ghost with wrinkles on their silver, illusory skin. A ghost wearing a ball gown, and a ghost wearing a flour sack with holes for the head and arms. A ghost with a magnificent crest of tiger-striped feathers. Children's ghosts, raptor and human alike.

Droplet took deep, slow breaths and clenched her hands together as something deep in the blood of this form told her brain, *this is wrong, this is dangerous, this will be you, you could be this, run, run.*

A neman in brocade robes appeared by her right shoulder, and she yelped; she tried to save face by turning the sound into an overexuberant sneeze.

When the mausoleum was full to bursting with dozens of ghosts, Azera unfolded her hands and stood up.

"Welcome. Thank you for responding," she said. She took a deep breath. Her eyes were back to normal, but they still shone from the tears that threatened to fall. "I need your help. Blood mages took my best friend, and she's on one of the noble islands. I can't search every island on my own. I need people who can travel everywhere unseen. I need people who can sense when there's magic in the air, who know how to find the strongest magic. I need people like you, or by the time I find her, it will be too late."

For a few moments, silence reigned. Droplet wondered if something had gone wrong with these ghosts. Then one, an older man in a robe of rags, snorted.

"Why should we help you?" he said, voice echoing with the same distant well-sound as Azera's grandmother. Some ghosts grumbled agreement.

Azera's jaw dropped.

"Yeah. You think we're giving you our time just because you can snap us up?"

"Someone doesn't know how things work around here," sang a child ghost. Azera's tears really were falling now, and she swallowed hard. Droplet stepped in front of her, anger rising. But Azera's grandmother spoke up first.

"Listen to yourselves! All of you!" She swept her arms wide, her impractical sleeves fluttering like real clothes. "What would your people say?"

"Our...people?" said the child ghost.

"Your people," the grandmother repeated. "I know better than to say your family, you hear? Not a one of us got through life without family letting us down. But your people—the ones you lived for, the ones you're still here for, maybe the ones you died for—what would they say if they saw you now?"

She paused. If she'd been alive, she'd have been panting, maybe pausing for air. But her chest didn't rise or fall with breath, nor did she sweat.

Into that stillness—the stillness of dozens of silent souls—she went on. "It's a rare thing, when you find a person like that. You'd do anything for your people. And that's what I'm doing for my granddaughter, and that's what she's doing for her friend. If you don't care for that, you can leave," she said, an addition that

Droplet thought was unwise, "but think of your person. Make them proud."

The older man who had first spoken nodded, the only movement in the breathless spirits. Then more nodded, or murmured, or stayed in place but looked sheepishly at their hovering feet that would never again touch the ground.

A few left, grumbling. But enough stayed. At least, Droplet hoped they would be enough.

"Thank you," Azera said, and Droplet couldn't tell if she addressed her grandmother or the ghosts. "Thank you all." She took a deep breath. "Here's what we need..."

A door swung open at the far end of the room. A masked trio strode in, and the leader said, "All right, girl, you were quite rude to one of my associates earlier. My friends and I wanted to have a little— *Holy Riverspawn preserve us!*" Two of the intruders, a raptor and a human, leapt for the door at the same time and collided. The speaker pointed a wand wildly from ghost to ghost.

The ghosts turned to look at them.

Azera folded her arms and slowly turned to face the intruders, eyes glimmering blue once more. "Do you mind?"

"Uh...sorry to intrude, ma'am. We'll be seeing ourselves out—"

Doors on the other end of the room sprang open as three bandits jumped in and had similar realizations about their catastrophic underestimation of the situation.

"Is that seeing yourselves out?" Azera asked with a chill to match the many dead of the room.

"Ma'am, forgive me, ma'am, but we can't coordinate across this building, our far-speech spells won't work in a dead place like this...uh, no offense to the dead, of course... Okay, everyone out, folks, this fine young woman is going to be left alone for her, uh, very important business pursuits."

Half a dozen bandits attempted to beat a hasty retreat while simultaneously projecting a façade of total confidence, as if jumping into a room and immediately exiting was exactly what they'd intended to do.

"Right," Azera said when they left. "So. Back to the plan..."

Azera, Droplet, and Azera's grandmother stayed behind in the mausoleum. After the rest of the ghosts had departed, Azera's grandmother flickered back to the spirit plane so Azera wouldn't "tucker herself out." Droplet and Azera were left to pass the time. They leaned on the wall, up against the markers of the dead. Droplet mentally apologized to Ervim Son of Eam and Lirvus Daughter of Umanira. They did not make comfortable backrests, and she fidgeted against the stone.

"So...what happened today?" Azera asked.

Knowing this question would come didn't make Droplet any happier at its arrival. "I told you. I got caught."

"Okay, suit yourself. But I'm here if you want to talk about it. You've been on edge since you got back." She paused. "More on edge than usual."

"Point of order: nothing about the last two days has been usual. For all you know, the rest of my life, I am a calm, collected, relaxed person."

"Aren't you a vigilante? Don't you do this sort of thing all the time?" Azera asked. She was smiling.

"People don't usually get in my head," Droplet admitted. When Azera didn't say anything, she continued, "Blood mages are so rare, and I've got bone charms that can deal with normal thought magic. And my memories...they were gone. Almost all of them. Memories are important." She stopped there, not sure how much she should tell. Nothing about the Enduring Archive, for sure. Nothing about the sacred mission of shapeshifter knowledge.

And part of her, traitorously, thought, *But none of that is really what's bothering you, is it? You haven't thought at all about what that loss would have meant for shapeshifterkind.*

Droplet pushed that part down, down, down. She didn't have to listen to it. But maybe she could finish this conversation without saying anything more. Maybe Droplet could trust that memories were important to humans, too, and so Azera would understand. Droplet turned to face Azera, who still waited after the pause, searching Droplet's face.

"Suddenly, it was all gone. And I didn't even know how much I had lost. But now I know," Droplet said.

"And it scares you now that you know, when it didn't before."

Droplet nodded.

"You found your way back, though," Azera said. She leaned in, earnest. "Even if they curse you again, I can get you out."

Right then would have been an excellent moment to tell Azera everything, tell Azera that she had brought Droplet back in more ways than one. But given the choice between having an open conversation with Azera and facing the cultists again, Droplet would have leapt for another round with the cultists.

Instead she said, with wry amusement, "Are you going to say 'I told you so'?"

"No, I'm just going to think it very hard and occasionally feel smug about it for the rest of my life," said Azera.

"That long?"

"It's a very emphatic 'I told you so.'"

Droplet laughed, and Azera smiled, a surprised, joyful smile.

"You should learn some of the shapeshifter language," Droplet said. "It would help if you knew some basic commands, like 'Run.'"

"Why would I need to know 'run'? You wouldn't be running away," Azera said, confused.

"So you can run," Droplet said.

"Oh!" Azera giggled for some reason. "Because I was picturing what would happen if I did tell you 'run'—you'd start charging right into the fray, wouldn't you?"

"I—"

"I'd say 'run,' and poof, you'd be a bear or something, galloping forward with murder in your eyes—"

"I don't murder!" Droplet protested, but she started laughing too. "Gods, and you'd be signing 'run' more and more frantically as I ran—"

"As a goose! That's it, you'd be a goose, of course!"

"Our enemies would be terrified," Droplet said.

"Our enemies would mock us."

"Making them all the more vulnerable as I *beat them into submission*," Droplet said.

Azera's eyes leaked tears now. She laughed too hard to speak, sending Droplet into another spasm of laughter in return.

Once she'd taken some deep breaths, Azera said, "You know I'm not running away either, right? I told you—I'm sticking with you."

Droplet sighed, at this point more reflex than anything else. She tried to ignore the reassurance and comfort Azera's words gave her. "I know," she said. "Let's do 'run' first, though."

"We have to, at this point," Azera said.

"Then I'll teach you some that we'll actually use."

Chapter Seventeen

The day everything went to hell came with no warning. Droplet, Yelarcha, and Rangitam played Chimney in the kitchen, the lowest level of the base. Moonshine, on cooking duty, trash-talked all three players with indiscriminate glee. More organization members—hybrids, mostly, but also a couple humans, a couple shapeshifters, and a griffin—drifted in and out, either to report to Yelarcha or to snag some food.

Pounding steps thudded on the ceiling above and echoed down the steps. The card players stood up, Droplet bracing herself to shift.

Forsyth raced down the steps. He'd stuck around for longer than most human operatives; it'd been nearly ten years since he first helped Droplet, and Droplet had never seen him this panicked.

"Go! Get out! You have to leave. They're coming," he panted without breaking stride, headed for the back door.

"Who's coming?" Yelarcha snapped, stepping between him and the door.

"The city watch, a bunch of nobles' personal guards, too many people," he said.

"What?!"

"How?"

"Here?!"

"How did they find us?" Yelarcha cawed, looking straight at Forsyth with the full intensity of her gaze.

He looked at the floor.

"Forsyth..." said Droplet.

Moonshine didn't speak; she moved. She bounded from the kitchen stove to pin Forsyth to the wall with one arm, still holding the knife she'd been using to chop garlic.

"What did you do?" Moonshine hissed.

"Moonshine!" Rangitam said.

"I had no choice!" Forsyth burst out. In the sudden silence within the kitchen, screams and thuds carried from upstairs. Moonshine pressed her arm more firmly against Forsyth's collarbone. "They threatened my wife! My children! I had to keep my family safe," he pleaded.

"So nice that you're the only one in this house with a family to keep safe," Moonshine said. She raised the knife to the level of Forsyth's face. "Oh, wait..."

The whole building shuddered. Moonshine reeled back, losing her balance. Yelarcha staggered. In the moment of relief, Forsyth pushed himself from the wall and fled out the back door.

Moonshine pursued him.

"Moonshine!" called Droplet.

"Rangitam, with me. We'll get Nedrud safely out. Sport, make sure everyone is evacuated," Yelarcha snapped. Droplet stared, dazed, at the spot where Forsyth had been.

She'd brought him here. She'd trusted him.

"*Droplet*," Yelarcha shouted.

Droplet snapped out of it. She'd been in tense situations before. She'd been calling herself a vigilante, hadn't she? She could do this.

She needed arms, so she stayed human as she raced up the stairs and straight into billowing smoke and crackling heat. The city-watch mages had blocked off the entrance with fire. But magical fire turned into real flames in a heartbeat without tight mage control.

Either the city watch was incompetent, or they wanted the place to burn.

Droplet ran from room to room calling names. In a second-floor washroom, she found a young owl hybrid, barely as high as her waist but too human-shaped to fly, trying to hide in the tub. Droplet picked him up and carried him to a window that overlooked a climbable tree, one she'd used many times for easy exit and entry. No time to see if he'd make it down—she had to keep searching.

She passed a couple humans trying to rescue books and files and *things*, and she shouted until they ran for the same window. She hustled into the room she'd called her own for nearly twenty years, and it was already burning, the fire licking up from underneath. Flames raced through the hallway, cutting off her exit. She dropped to the ground, under the smoke, but the floor was hot on her hands. What could she shift to? What could she be? Did she have some form that could handle the fire and the watch and the destruction and the betrayal?

Every breath made her cough.

Hard to breathe.

Hard to decide.

Hard to act.

The flames died suddenly, and she could hear tramping feet. The watch must have decided they'd burned enough.

Then, closer, she heard paws.

A lioness burst into the room, fur singed and whiskers frazzled. **DROPLET!** Moss said. Droplet looked up, bleary, and coughed smoke. **My Droplet, my Droplet, quickly**, said Moss, running in circles around her, punctuating her words with nudges and low growls. Droplet stood up unsteadily. She placed her hand on the lioness's shoulders for support. **I can carry you**, Moss said.

The shift to cat form felt like falling, the walls and bed and dressers and mirror rushing away and growing until they weren't made for her anymore.

Moss picked her up in her jaws, and they fled into the city, away from the wreckage, the watch, and the flames.

Chapter Eighteen

Droplet had time to teach Azera many useful words of the shapeshifter language in the human, quadruped, and bird dialects, before the ghosts began to return. On a night like tonight, magic abounded even more than usual. Islands with bespelled decorations, security systems, and other magical features had spared no expense for enchanted midsummer decorations to complement the place. The first dozen ghosts who came back, reporting from three of the six islands, could only agree on a "maybe" at best.

Then a child ghost came back, from a fourth island, to report the island silent yet so suffused with magic that they hadn't been able to get within ten feet of the shoreline. Azera and Droplet quizzed the other ghosts on everything they knew about the island. Nothing much, which in itself was a kind of answer. Nobody had been a servant there. Nobody had visited. Nobody had heard wild rumors from a relative or friend.

It seemed Hawthorn Island was their target.

By the time the ghosts had reported back, night had fallen even on this shortest night. Droplet guessed it was ten in the evening.

In the darkness, Droplet became a roc and flew them. From high overhead, Hell Street on the main island blazed like a river of sunlight. The outlying islands sparkled like stars in the night-black sea. Echoes of laughter and music floated into the air, loud enough to be heard over the wind rushing past Droplet's ears as she labored to fly. On the other plane, she knew, ghosts flew with her, at least to the edge of the island.

At Hawthorn Island, silence reigned. The small island held only a grove of trees, a three-story manor, and a few dark outbuildings. Lights shone within curtained windows, and a faded illumination spell on the manor's façade outlined a rose in faint, glowing red lines like wounds.

Droplet was not impressed.

Once they'd landed and Droplet had shifted, she muttered, "If you want to be subtle about your death cult's hidden base, do you cover the front in lines of blood? Do you?"

"Hasn't been a problem for them yet," Azera said.

"You can get away with anything if people think you're rich," Droplet said, to a vigorous nod of agreement.

Azera led them around the house. Thanks to her visits to the manor where Harra worked, and thanks to her casual infiltration of multiple parties, Azera had some idea of how these kinds of houses were usually set up. Though the Sacarian houses had some architectural differences, rich Sacarians, like rich Ninuthenites, wanted their servants to go in and out of the house as unobtrusively as possible. That entrance would probably be the least secure.

Droplet became a sparrow and snuggled into a pocket of the serving uniform Azera had stolen...gods, was it only yesterday morning? No doubt magical alarms protected the building, but Azera's necromantic nature would ensure they didn't notice her. Azera bundled up Droplet's clothes to keep them handy as they explored the building.

Azera shivered as she approached the door. Droplet, on her shoulder, felt a faint tremor in the air: powerful magic. Azera tapped the doorknob hesitantly; when nothing happened, she tried the knob.

Locked.

She withdrew a few hairpins from her hair and picked the lock before Droplet had time to be concerned that they'd prepared for blood mages and not locked doors.

The door opened into a bland hallway of featureless walls. Azera slipped in and slowly eased the door shut behind her. Small light-stones in the ceiling cast a faint orange glow over the hallway—barely enough for Droplet to see Azera's feet.

Azera and Droplet together peeked into the first room they came to, on the left. Even as a sparrow, the smell of some floral perfume assaulted her nose. The room was small and, from its position in the house, probably served as a servant's room, but tapestries hung on the unassuming walls. A wardrobe inlaid with mother-of-pearl willow designs stood on one side. A thick Nortakian wool rug in vibrant sky-blues and greens covered most of the floor.

"Sacarian servants aren't…wildly richer than normal servants, right?" Azera whispered.

Droplet shook her head.

The next servant's chamber was similarly opulent, as was the next. Azera shuddered and rubbed at her skin as they went—there must be background magic throughout the manor. Unsurprising. Droplet wondered what the rest of the house looked like. And where were the people?

They reached a small stair on their right and headed up.

Light spilled out from the plain and unassuming door to the next landing, but no sound—unmistakable signs of a magical barrier. Azera hissed as her hand touched the door handle. The spell must be potent, to affect her. She gritted her teeth and turned the handle, leaning her weight into it.

The spell broke abruptly, sending Azera stumbling forward as the handle turned freely and the door swung open. Shouts and crashes poured through.

Droplet got an impression of gold and red before someone tackled Azera to the ground, taking Droplet with them.

"Blood and bones!" Azera swore.

"We've got one! We've got one!" the wolf pinning her shouted. Droplet flapped madly against Azera's pocket, trying to free herself.

"They're back already?!" exclaimed a humanoid hybrid covered in iridescent green scales. More hybrids were rushing over now, armed with chair legs, picture frames, and fans.

"We're not blood mages," Azera gasped.

" 'We'?" said the wolf, and then, "They're more of them!" to the half-dozen advancing hybrids.

Finally, Droplet burst out of Azera's pocket. She flew enough to get space, then became a griffin.

"We're here to help," she said, but shouts of surprise drowned her words. The hybrids at least stopped rushing them. The wolf kept Azera pinned. "We're here to help!" she repeated, even though she wanted to simply screech. "Get off her, already," she snapped at the wolf.

"Why should we trust you?" the wolf demanded, hackles starting to rise.

"I'm Harra's friend," Azera said, voice remarkably mild for someone whose face was only a few feet from a wolf's jaws. "Just get Harra. She'll vouch for us, and then we can all get out of here." Ahhh, right, this was Azera's "desperately pleasant" voice, the last stand of attempted civility before she broke out the necromancy.

Droplet realized her hackles were bristling and took deep breaths. *These are scared people. We will all work together soon.*

The wolf stepped off.

Azera slowly, slowly pushed herself up, wincing as she put pressure on her wrists.

Someone must have gone to find Harra, because the sound of running feet echoed around the frozen hybrids, Droplet, and Azera, fading as whoever was running drew farther away from them. The hybrids who were more human than not wore fine clothes, though most of them were rumpled and torn. The room they stood in looked like some kind of sitting room—plush rugs of Nortakian reds and purples, red marble pillars carved with floral reliefs, massive paintings on the walls, a fireplace that had been gilded within an inch of its life. Overturned chairs littered the sides of the room, many of them missing their legs, presumably also gilded.

Shouts and crashes carried from distant rooms now that this one was still.

"I'm Azera Carpenter, from Ninuthen," said Azera into the silence.

"And I'm Droplet," said Droplet.

"I'm Whali from Humberthen," the scaly human volunteered.

"Don't trust them yet," the wolf sighed, face turning skyward in exasperation.

Soon, running footsteps approached again from the distant chaos. Different footsteps this time, lighter and faster.

A gray tabby hybrid skidded into the room, nearly falling over the edge of the rug before leaping toward Azera.

"Azera!"

Harra slammed into Azera and clung, tail lashing wildly. Azera hugged her back, both of them swaying with the impact. Droplet told herself not to cry, though she felt weak on her feet too.

They'd made it.

They'd found her.

She'd succeeded.

"It's you! You're really here!" Azera cried.

"Why are *you* here? This is *so dangerous*."

"What, like I was going to just leave you? You gave Grandma all these details—"

"So you could talk to, I don't know, some kind of authority! There are people who handle these sorts of things!"

"I did," Azera said, briefly taking one hand away from the embrace to gesture in Droplet's general direction. "And then I came too, to make sure."

"*Azera*," Harra said with fond exasperation. She loosened her claws some from Azera's back and peered at Droplet with wide eyes.

"Hi. We, ah, met, briefly," said Droplet, inclining her feathered head in greeting.

"Ohh, the shapeshifter! Hello! I'm glad you're all right!"

"I'm glad *you're* all right. You're the one I last saw charging at them with nothing but some splinters," said Droplet.

"What's going on here? We've got to get you out," Azera said.

"We're trying to break out," Harra said.

"Most of the cultists are out celebrating, so we subdued the ones who were left behind. But the doors and windows are sealed," said the wolf.

"The way we came is still open—can we get everyone out that way? How many of you are there?" Azera asked.

The assembled crowd looked at the open door. Some raised their makeshift weapons again. The wolf snarled.

"The cultists live down there. They tell us they live like servants because we're the real heroes," Whali, the scaly human, explained.

Droplet snorted and said, "Typical."

"It's a servants' hall, all right, but the rooms are absurd. It smells like someone doused their whole floor in that perfume your boss likes, Harra, and they've got...fancy curtains, I don't know what the name is, but you'd recognize them. It's all 'rich people' stuff down there," Azera said.

Shouts of outrage echoed around the sitting room. A hawk hybrid perched on a fallen chair near Droplet started describing exactly what he'd do to the cultists in vivid detail. A hybrid with a human's upper body, lion's legs, and a ragged gold mane declared that the rooms and hallway were probably filled with magical traps, and thus any escape attempt that way was a fool's errand. In the hubbub, Harra asked Azera, "Do you think you can open the front door?"

"I'll try, but I don't know if I can. This door nearly stopped me, and I don't know if I can get us help more than once," Azera said. With everything that had happened that day, Droplet spent a confused moment wondering who would be coming to help before she remembered, *right, ghosts.* Azera darted glances around the nearby captives, still in an uproar, before she added, "Summoning anyone across a distance and across this much magic is like dragging a lake uphill. I can't even talk with Grandmother from here."

"I'll get everyone rounded up. You try the door. If that doesn't work, we'll have to go out through the servants' hall," Harra declared. Harra pointed the way, and Azera strode off. Harra clapped her hands together, surveyed the room, and yowled, "QUIET!"

The echoes of the yowl bounced off the pillars and walls in the ensuing silence.

"Azera's going to try to break down the front door. If that doesn't work, we go out this way. Clawhame, Whali, round up everyone on this floor. Gak, get anyone who's upstairs." The wolf and scaly human ran out of the sitting room; the hawk took to the air and followed. Droplet oriented herself toward the hallway Azera had taken. Harra continued, "You—um—"

"Droplet."

"Droplet, can you check on Azera?"

She didn't need to be asked twice. She bounded away, taking savage pleasure in scuffing her claws against the floors as she ran.

Droplet caught up with Azera in moments; Azera was striding toward the door with the same determination that she'd shown marching into a strange shapeshifter's home and demanding help. When she was still five steps away from it, she slowed. Each step moved like molasses. When she couldn't drag her feet anymore, Azera stretched her arm out, gasping. Droplet leapt toward her and smacked paws-first into an invisible wall. She landed on her feet, shook herself, and stretched. Nothing had been harmed but her dignity, and Azera didn't look to have noticed, too focused on trying to press forward.

Azera staggered backward and gasped for air like she'd been drowning. Through the shuddering breaths, she said, "Downstairs. This won't work."

Halting, stumbling, Azera tried to run back to the sitting room where Harra and the others assembled. Wings partly raised in case she needed to break Azera's fall, Droplet loped alongside her. But as Azera continued, her gait evened, and by the time they reached the others, she'd regained her footing.

Murmurs of conversation filled the tense sitting room as Harra and a half-bear hybrid did a headcount. "Any luck?" Harra asked Azera as they re-entered the room.

Azera shook her head.

"Then we go out the back way," the half-bear declared. "Clawhame?"

The wolf ran down the stairs, leading the pack. Others followed at the same clip, the crowd moving out as fast as possible. Nobody jostled each other, Droplet noted approvingly. Harra joined Droplet by Azera's side as the rest of the captives raced past. As soon as Azera had caught her breath, the three of them joined the rush.

In the narrow hallways of the service quarters, the pounding of feet on stone turned the space into a reverberating drum. The hallways that had been so eerily empty when Droplet and Azera arrived were almost unrecognizable when filled with fear and sweat and people.

The frontrunners in the group stopped well short of the door and started directing the others to make way for Azera as she continued wiggling forward. Droplet itched to move forward with her, but the space was too cramped, so she stayed back.

Azera was halfway to the front of the group when the doorknob turned.

No time to react. Nowhere to hide.

The door opened, and laughter and chatter flowed in. The

cultists had been celebrating, after all. Then the ones at front saw the captives.

"What the—?"

Half the captives turned to flee, crashing into Azera and knocking her against the wall. A few charged the blood mages. One mage, quicker on the uptake, drew a knife and slashed the back of her hand in a practiced motion, bellowing in a language Droplet had never heard. The charging captives staggered to the ground.

Azera caught her breath and placed her hands together. At the same time, the wall next to the door melted like ice over a fire, a second opening appearing so more blood mages could pour in. Azera's grandmother and three other ghosts sprang into being, even fainter than usual, and Azera staggered into Harra, exhausted.

Droplet couldn't fly in such a cramped space, but she could bound over the heads of the hybrids. Using all the reflexes at her disposal to avoid landing on the people who'd fallen in the first wave, she leapt into the gap that had opened between the cultists and the captives.

More faint ghosts appeared.

More blood mages raised bleeding hands.

Behind Droplet, Azera screamed.

Time seemed to stop as Droplet took in everything. The hallway had expanded to be Droplet's entire universe. Far behind her, the captives fled down corridors too narrow for the flood of people, with no way to get out. In front of her, the blood mages—she could see past the first row, now, and there were nearly as many blood mages in that crowd as captives in the house. Some bled. Some drew weapons. Above her, the faint, ineffective ghosts; below and immediately behind her, the collapsed and collapsing captives, trying to fight.

And now, Azera, crying out.

Droplet wanted to become a roc, an elephant, a rhinoceros, something to bring this whole manor down around her ears as she trampled the cultists. But she was hemmed in by people she was supposed to protect. How could she protect them when they kept getting in her way? A spitting cobra—no, the blood mages would get her before she managed to spray more than half a dozen of them. A goose—they'd stop a goose even sooner, and they'd have her trapped. She didn't know what they did to coerce people into giving them memories, but she and Azera would be two more victims soon enough—

Wait.

Azera still screamed.

Droplet became a lion—barely a shift at all—and she roared. A lion's roar travelled from the ears directly back in time through thousands of years, back to when all peoples that considered themselves "civilized" didn't even have fire to keep out the night. A lion's roar announced to all in earshot that, for all their illusions, the lion knew what you really were: prey.

But most importantly, a lion's roar was *loud.*

The blood mages stopped moving. The injured stopped moaning. Azera stopped screaming. In that silence, Droplet changed into the Dalere human.

"I'd like to negotiate," she said.

The blood mages stared at her. She met their gaze coolly. She realized after a few moments of standoff that perhaps some of them were staring because she was naked, and gods, raptors and humans were so weird.

The mages at the front shuffled aside to make way for Isna. Droplet spotted Solvim in the crowd too. Like many others, his mouth was still agape.

"You are outnumbered and overpowered in every way. I'm quite curious what you plan to bargain with," said Isna.

"First, I have questions," said Droplet.

"Go on."

"Your ceremony requires a certain number of sacrifices, yes?"

"A simplistic description, but yes."

"And is that measured by number of memories or number of participants?"

"Droplet..." said Azera.

"Memories," said Isna.

"Excellent," Droplet said. She waved her hands, trying to encompass all the captives with a single gesture. She didn't let herself think, not for a second. "Let all these people go. Keep me instead."

"DROPLET!"

She ignored Azera. Isna did too.

"Think about it. I don't even know the half of what you did to get these people here, but you know you're bending 'willing' sacrifice until it almost breaks. Think of what you'll get with a freely offered trade," said Droplet.

"This sounds like a trick," one of the other cultists said.

Isna held up a hand for silence. The feathers of her arm glistened with blood. "You realize you're volunteering to give dozens of memories away in this ritual?"

"Do you know how long shapeshifters live?" Droplet bluffed. Isna cocked her head to the side and straightened, gaining some height over Droplet, and she peered down at her, nostrils widening as if she was sniffing for a lie. Droplet tried to project the confidence she'd seen in Moss, in her own mother, in other shapeshifters who had lived for hundreds of years and knew what they were doing. Isna settled back down into her more natural posture.

"And why should we let the others go instead of keeping all of you?" Isna asked.

"Because you think you're heroes, don't you? That's the whole point of this charade, why your prisoners sleep in fancy bedrooms while you take servants' cells. That's why you talked about this as such a great honor for the people you drag from their homes and lock up. That's why you didn't kill me this morning. You think you're good people. And if you're good people—really good people—you know this isn't right. You've got your rationalizations, your logic, your talks about how this ritual keeps the whole world safe, and what does a little bit of evil to a few little lives matter, really, compared to the world? But you know that it matters, deep down. And if you want to be the kind of people your precious guardians would be proud of fighting for, you are going to *let these people go.*"

Droplet did not break eye contact.

Isna let her words hang in the air for agonizing seconds. Then she nodded. "Let the others go," she said.

"But—Isna—"

"Let them take the boats. Keep your weapons leveled on them until they're out of sight. Shoot if they try anything. But our shapeshifter friend is right. Our honored sacrifices have always been resentful. If they do not appreciate the honor, we do not need to keep them."

I plan to be extremely resentful, Droplet thought. Aloud, she said, "Someone get the people who ran into the house. Make sure everyone gets out." Someone assented. She didn't look away from Isna to see who it was.

"And could someone get this...shapeshifter...some clothes?" said Isna, similarly holding Droplet's gaze. Nobody moved. "Step up, step up. They're not going to hurt you. I think that would be an unfortunate move for all parties involved."

"I have her clothes," Azera said.

"Come on, then. Everyone can move now," the raptor said. She and Droplet continued to hold each other's gaze as those around them began to shuffle into motion.

The captives began to leave, led by Clawhame, slow as fawns taking their first steps. The blood mages formed a corridor to let them pass, hands on weapons or touching wounds they'd already opened.

Droplet held her ground until she heard Azera's stomping reach her. She turned and reached for her clothes, trading Isna's cool assessment for Azera's blazing fury.

"You can't do this," Azera said.

"Clearly I can. I'm not even going to die," Droplet said.

"Volunteering for giving up your memories in eternal captivity is still bad!"

"I can take care of myself. I told you I work best alone, didn't I?" Droplet said. She had no idea how she'd get out of this, but that wasn't the point. "You do what you came here for. Get your friend out. You're right, you know. I can't get them out alone."

Azera radiated fury. Droplet was mostly sure that Azera was angry at the cultists, not her. Mostly.

Harra came up and rested a furred hand on Azera's shoulder. She nodded at Droplet. "Thank you," she said. "There are not words to thank you enough, but I thank you anyway."

"I did what I had to," Droplet said. "Hurry up and leave, yes? Don't let them follow you."

"Azera's got us," Harra said. Azera hadn't moved, though she looked almost as desperate now as when she'd first shown up on Droplet's doorstep. Harra shook her. "Everyone else has left. Come on, Az."

Azera nodded once. Then she flung her arms around Droplet. Droplet barely had time to put her arms around her in return and pat her back before she broke away. Head held high and fists clenched, Azera turned and walked down the aisle of armed cultists.

She left.

Droplet was alone with the cult.

Chapter Nineteen

The cultists insisted that they wouldn't use any magic on her before the ceremony. Droplet believed them; using magic could interfere with the ritual's "willing sacrifice" requirement. They also were nice and polite, presumably because they wanted to believe in the lie of their own goodness. They offered her whatever she wanted from the pantry, and she took them up on it, eating day-old rolls and handfuls of tangy marshberries.

Solvim took her on a tour of the mansion, nattering away about the artifacts of the cult's history on display in the rooms. This cult leader's contributions to the arts. That cult leader's generosity to the poor. That painter's genius. This furniture's cost. A mismatch of five centuries' ideas of opulence jumbled together like the collection of the world's wealthiest magpie. Amidst the gilding sat signs of life from all the people who'd recently fled, like the room where the silk bedsheets were askew. In another room, five hands of cards had been left, mid-game, on the mahogany table. Soap stains bedecked a pink marble washroom.

"They really didn't respect this place, did they?" Solvim said, shaking his head in dismay.

Droplet punched him in the back. She didn't even bother to shift shapes to do it.

Solvim whirled on her. "What was that for?"

"It's a prison, you mosquito. It doesn't matter how you dress it up."

Solvim was much terser during the rest of the tour.

When Droplet had a moment's peace, she tried to pick the memories she could bear to lose.

Mother would be so furious if she knew, she thought. That's why thinking had been a bad idea. That's why she had to jump into this. She'd done what she'd done.

She hadn't been to the Enduring Archive. She'd never shared what she knew with history. The things she'd seen and done would be lost forever. The shapeshifters would have holes in their records. What if this doomed the shapeshifter mission? What if, thousands of years from now, shapeshifterkind tried to return to the stars and the stars said "No"?

Stop it. That's nonsense. There's always going to be stuff we don't experience on this world or things we forget, Droplet told herself firmly. Her internal voice sounded like Moss. Droplet'd had so many questions for Moss back in the early organization days; Moss had always been there when Droplet worried about what the archivists would think. What the stars thought, looking down on them. In Droplet's lowest moments, when she couldn't sleep, Moss would become a shaggy snow leopard, wrap her tail around Droplet, and groom her until she dozed off clutching Moss's fur.

Those were memories Droplet wouldn't give up. Surely she could give the cult boring memories. Would it be better to give them memories from her childhood with her colony? That way other shapeshifters would have been there. Someone else would remember those times. The archive would see them.

Maybe if I ask nicely, the guardians will take the memories to the archive for me, Droplet thought, and the absurdity of it made her laugh, and laugh, and laugh because she'd be dead before she let those cultists see her cry.

The sacrifice would be held in the ballroom.

Unlike the rest of the house, the ballroom held only one piece of furniture: the altar. Not to say that the room wasn't ostentatious; when the cultists escorting Droplet opened the double doors into the room, she faced floor-to-ceiling stained-glass windows depicting the guardians and their eventual triumph over the demons. Feathery humanoids with rainbow wings stood atop a writhing, dark-green mass with no specific form, only lots of teeth and narrow red eyes. Each panel moved in slow, silent animation. In the central panel, one guardian brought a sword down on a demon face and one sliced at a receding tendril, moving at molasses speed. In the night, with no light from outside, even the guardians were murky and dark.

The walls to either side of the doors looked to be dirty plaster. Droplet took a closer look at the dark markings and had to stare for almost a minute before she made out tiny letters. The cultists had written names—thousands of names, maybe tens of thousands.

"The names go back to the very day the guardians routed the demons from our world," a blood mage said. "We haven't forgotten. We'll write yours down at the end of the ceremony." She pointed down the wall—very far down—where the texture made by the names stopped and only white plaster was left.

"I don't have a name yet," Droplet said. "Not really." She never would if she didn't get out of here. But no, she wouldn't think about that tonight. She had all the time in the world to escape. As bleak as things looked now, they'd be better tomorrow. They had to be.

"It is time," Isna announced.

Droplet stood by the altar, facing the windows. The blood mages had changed into matching clothes: brown, shapeless garments that may well have been sewn-together potato sacks. Isna's clothes were the same as the rest. Droplet steeled herself for having to listen to interminable speeches about humility from rich people in a world-class ballroom, an experience sure to be more painful than the actual blood loss. Maybe she could immediately get rid of that memory.

As the mages formed a circle nearly as wide as the ballroom, she became an elephant. Tile cracked under her feet, and she heard some murmurs and gasps around her. Whether the reactions were a response to her change or about the damage to a priceless floor, she couldn't say and didn't care. She would need to lose a lot of blood as they yanked away memories. She wanted to be prepared.

Isna clasped her hands and looked around at the group. "Brethren, friends, honored guests. Thank you for coming...some of you from across the ocean, even! As the time draws near and our guardians draw closer to the world—"

"STOP RIGHT THERE."

Droplet flapped her ears and trumpeted in surprise. The blood mages spun to face the doors. Droplet couldn't turn as quickly, but she'd recognize that voice anywhere. She lumbered around until she saw Azera. Her face was set. She was alone.

What are you doing?! Droplet thought.

"What is the meaning of this?" Isna snapped. "We had a deal!"

"*You* may have had a deal, but I cannot possibly tell you how little I care about that. You're letting Droplet go, now. Throw away your own memories if you care about your guardians so much." Azera moved as she talked, pacing like a circling tiger as she slowly made her way around the giant perimeter of mages.

"And we should listen to you because...?" Isna said, leaning forward, curling her claws against the stone of the altar.

"You know who I am. You know what I can do. If I fill this room with ghosts, no magic is getting back to your precious guardians, is it?"

"We can simply remove you from this hall," Isna said.

"Try it and I'll struggle. Sure, you may get me out of the hall, but can you guarantee you're not going to spill even a single drop of my very, very unwilling blood? Because I'm no mage, but I think even one drop will poison the entire spell. Oh, and you're running short on time."

"Don't you understand what we're doing here, stupid girl? We're saving this whole blighted world from destruction!" said an elderly raptor in the crowd.

"The guardians need us!" another cultist called.

"Give them your own cursed minds, then, if you believe in them so much!" Azera snapped. Droplet kept turning to face Azera as she continued her slow progression around the circle. She couldn't have looked away, not for anything. Azera was walking in front of the stained-glass guardians, now, as the glacial rise and fall of slashing swords continued behind her. Every cultist was trained on her, some with hands raised, all armed—they'd come with knives, gods, of course, because they'd all need to shed their blood anyway.

"And who will carry on our work if we destroy ourselves now, hm?" Isna said.

Not a single person turned to look at Isna. She got some shouts of agreement, but the mages didn't break focus.

"I don't give a damn, personally. That's a problem for you to solve," Azera said. The room broke into shouts. The circle wavered as mages stepped out of line, as if Azera was a magnet pulling them in. All of them watching—

—and none of them watching Droplet.

Droplet could see Azera's hands as she circled ever closer, cultists in front of her and wide, wide glass behind her. Her hands beat the air in front of her torso. The shapeshifter language.

Run.

Trumpeting, Droplet barreled forward, the altar barely a bump against her massive legs as she careened toward the windows. She lowered her head as she charged, and Azera shouted "Yes!"—a shout that cut into an "OOF" as Droplet snagged her around the waist with her trunk, tucking her safely beneath the elephant body.

Glass crashed around Droplet's head, and then she was free.

Fresh sea air buffeted her, blowing in from beyond these ghastly islands. Impeccably manicured hedges and geometric flower beds smashed under her giant feet.

"Left, left," Azera shouted. Droplet obliged. In her path sat a marble fountain of the guardians inlaid with firefly-like lights, a row of statues of woodland creatures with soppy expressions, and a gate that had done its best to make lacework out of metal.

The blood mages poured out of the gap that had once been a window. Ghosts appeared around Droplet, solid now—well, as solid as ghosts would ever be—and Azera shuddered in her trunk, gasping for air like she'd just raced a cheetah.

Azera had said this would cost her, hadn't she? How much?

Can't panic now, Droplet thought.

Droplet lifted Azera high above her head and stampeded. Stonework crunched and metal creaked. The bent remains of the metal gate attempted to clutch her leg until she kicked it into the darkness.

The island sloped down toward a rocky shore.

Harra waited for them by the beach, leaping up and down. "Be a roc, be a roc, we sent all the boats away already," she babbled, puffed up to twice her normal size. Droplet set Azera down like thin glass and changed forms, the ground shrinking even farther away. Harra leaped at her, and Droplet screeched. The half-cat clung to her feathers and climbed up to her back like she was scaling a tree. Her claws dug into Droplet's skin, but Droplet felt it would be uncharitable to complain.

"Pick up Azera and whatever happens, don't let her go. She might faint. She said she wouldn't, but I don't believe her."

Droplet whirled her head—stars, what a relief to have reflexes like this after being an elephant—to fix Harra with a one-eyed glare.

"Have *you* been able to stop her doing what she wants? It never gets easier," Harra said.

Droplet cawed, took off, then swooped back to grab Azera as delicately as she could. She couldn't talk to them in this form, so she couldn't tell Harra that she had read Droplet's glare all wrong.

As if I would let Azera go, Droplet scoffed.

The sounds of the blood mages faded into the distance.

"Head for the nuns Azera was talking about. All of us are going there."

Droplet wheeled left toward the lights of Sacarus's main island. Far to her right, in the northeastern part of the bay, the midsummer midnight fireworks began, showers of purple and gold and red and white lighting their way back.

Chapter Twenty

When Droplet showed up at the Church of the Eternal Flame after midnight with a half-conscious Azera and a few dozen hybrids, Mother Enneth didn't bat an eye. Droplet, human once more, stood in the secret warehouse entrance with Harra, Azera, Rangitam, and the elderly nun. Hybrids shuttled back and forth around them, ushered by nuns in varying states of confusion.

"I negotiated with the warehouse owners while you were out. We have bedrolls laid out and a handsomely paid-off security force watching over the building," Mother Enneth said to Droplet, as if the shapeshifter had been out to the market and not breaking into and out of a blood mage enclave.

"Does anyone need our room? We could take bedrolls," Azera mumbled.

Mother Enneth eyed the trio. Droplet and Harra supported Azera between them—she'd not been able to so much as stand since returning. Rangitam hovered behind Droplet as if she, too, would collapse at any moment. Ridiculous. Droplet was fine.

"You're keeping a bed," Mother Enneth declared, "but I'll add extra bedrolls so you don't go feeling guilty about it."

"What about the Eyes? The cult?" Droplet said. She started to gesture as she talked, swayed, nearly dropped Azera, and decided against it.

"They'll still be around tomorrow after you've had a good night's sleep," Mother Enneth said. She yawned. "Goodness me. I should carry an extra cane around to shake at people. Go to bed! Go! My nuns will take care of everyone until morning."

"And the hired security," Rangitam said.

"Yes, yes, and the hired security."

The four of them made it to the bedroom through hallways packed with freed hybrids and the church's usual midsummer boarders. Droplet couldn't spare a thought for them; they were merely obstacles between where Azera was now and getting Azera to a place where she could lie down. And perhaps Droplet could also lie down, for a bit? Should she keep watch? She could keep watch lying down, maybe?

The closed door of their room nearly defeated her. Did she have hands right now? She did, didn't she? But Azera needed those hands. She stood blinking before Rangitam leaned over and turned the knob.

"Go to bed," he declared, shoving her, Azera, and Harra in.

Getting Azera onto the bed took much more of a collective effort than Droplet had expected. Somehow, by the time they succeeded, everyone but Rangitam was lying down. Harra tucked herself into a ball. Azera sprawled on the wall side, already asleep. Droplet blinked blearily at Rangitam.

"You're safe here," he said. "You did it, Droplet."

Droplet trusted Rangitam, but surely she should be prepared. What about the Eyes? What if the cult came back?

She yawned deeply.

I'll have to shift now. Ready to go in an instant. Wake up and fight on a moment's notice.

She shifted into a goose. Distantly, she registered Rangitam placing his face into his furry palm. She didn't care.

Without bothering to shake free of her human clothes, she tucked her head under a wing and went to sleep.

Droplet woke up with her head still tucked under her wing. She lay in a nest of cloth—clothes?—and everything hurt. Her immediate impulse was to spring up and start biting everything, but...she did hurt. And the nest was very cozy. There were blankets around her.

Maybe this was time to try that "restraint" and "knowing your limits" method that Moss talked about. Surely people who had made such a nice nest did not plan to immediately kill her. She slowly untucked and raised her neck.

She lay on the bed of a vaguely familiar stone room. Harra and Rangitam stood nearby, talking softly. Droplet turned her neck back toward the bed and found Azera blinking away sleep. Droplet watched her wake up. Because she wanted to make sure she was okay, of course. Someone had to look out for her.

Azera spotted her watching, and her face broke into one of those rare, unhesitant smiles that lit up the world.

"Good. You're both awake!" said Harra.

Droplet twisted her neck around as Rangitam scooped her up into an undignified hug. Droplet honked.

"*You're* awake," Azera said to Harra. "How are you? Is everyone safe?"

"Safe as a cub in its mother's den. Mother Enneth and Rangitam are miracle workers, I'll tell you that," said Harra.

"Oh please," Rangitam demurred.

"Have you slept enough?" Azera said to Harra.

"You know me—I'll take naps." She certainly seemed awake enough, her ears perked and eyes wide, taut with energy. "Come on, let's get you fed."

Whether it was the hired security, the excessive bone wards of the church, or the cult members giving up, no attack had come in the night—nor had a raid from the Eyes.

Droplet shifted to her first Dalere form. She'd left the room by the time she realized that this form wasn't the same one she'd been in when she arrived at the nunnery—the too-short clothes should have been a clue—but by then it was too late. Harra led Droplet and Azera to the common room, which was even more crowded than the night before. Mother Enneth sat like a queen holding court on a chair nearly hidden by mismatched pillows.

"Dalere, Azera, my children! Come sit a spell with an old woman. Have some breakfast," Mother Enneth commanded. So she'd seen right through the change in human form, then. Droplet let herself be ushered into an empty chair. Harra and Rangitam joined the whirlwind throng. Mother Enneth clasped her gnarled hands together and beamed at the two of them.

"By now, I do believe half the city is talking about the Cult of the Endless War. The finger-pointing and accusations have started already, of course, but I wondered if either of you had any guidance on who we can throw to the wolves."

"Uh," Azera said.

"Ah, forgive an old woman for getting ahead of herself, my dear. Let me start from the beginning. My beloved flock has been spreading news of the *shocking* discovery of this sacrificial cult and spree of kidnappings, right in our midst! The horror! The revelers last night were quite receptive to the tale. It helped, of course, that a bedraggled, haunted pack of hybrids had stumbled through the street. Exceptionally visible. I commend you."

"That part was unintentional," said Droplet.

"Yes, Rangitam tells me you prefer the 'direct action' part of this life to the, ah, strategic aspects," Mother Enneth said, voice full of fondness, like a grandmother admiring a grandchild's first work of art. Droplet felt...warm. A bit patronized, yes, but in an old, familiar way, like Nedrud ruffling her hair. She didn't mind, so much, that Rangitam had told Mother Enneth more about her.

That was new.

Mother Enneth continued, "The city is in an uproar. We've already spoken with those you rescued to glean information on those responsible, but I wanted to hear from you before we begin our latest round of gossiping in the streets."

"Three different noble houses have already turned in rival houses for supporting the blood cult. Three! And it's not even noon," Rangitam added as he and Harra returned bearing breakfast trays. His wagging tail thumped against Droplet's arm. "The nobles and the tourists are calling for the Eyes to arrest the blood cult yesterday."

"My sisters say we've had some people questioning what good the Eyes are if they couldn't even stop this," Mother Enneth said. She radiated satisfaction as she sipped tea. "What an excellent crack to drive a wedge into. I commend you both."

Droplet regretted choosing a human form whose cheeks could show a radiating blush. "How is everyone getting home?"

"I'm working on that. With help from the nuns, of course," said Harra. Droplet looked askance at her. Harra caught the look and said, "It's been a *trying* few days. Logistics soothe me. And I am an exemplary planner."

"Like your plan to charge at blood mages armed with a couple of wooden boards?" Droplet said.

Harra sniffed. "An excellent plan that worked out perfectly. I'll thank you not to tease."

Now Droplet was confused. "They captured you," she said.

"Yes, well, it seemed like the best outcome in the circumstances. Look at it from my perspective. You were clearly competent enough to find me and the others, which also meant you knew much more about the situation than me. When the blood mages had you trapped, distracting them was only logical. Either you'd get away *and* free me—unlikely—or, at minimum, you'd get away and live to carry on your noble quest for justice. And I was right," Harra said smugly.

Droplet gaped.

"And if I ask Grandmother about this, she'll of course agree that you had this all thought out, and it wasn't a hare-brained moment of reckless heroism," said Azera.

"She will if she knows what's good for her," said Harra.

Still processing, Droplet leaned forward, elbows on the table and chin on her hands. Azera patted her back, and then her hand came to rest between Droplet's shoulder blades.

"You're not the only one at this table who can be self-sacrificing," Azera said.

"Ah, youth," Mother Enneth said. "Now…shall we talk more about these cultists?"

After the talk, Droplet, Harra, and Rangitam went to a public far-speak bank, flanked by a few of the burliest security guards from the nunnery.

Far-speak banks contained rows and rows of doorless stone stalls, the entryways muffled with air spells to give some semblance of privacy. The discs in this one were almost as good as the sphere-encased one Isna had used back at the tavern. *They must make great money off the tourists*, Droplet thought. The discs had been spelled to connect with any other far-speak discs, allowing for any person to complete the appropriate incantation whether or not they had magic. Droplet spoke the necessary words and heard the disc come to life, the ambient noise of her own manor in Ninuthen drifting through.

"Moss?" she called.

Running footsteps echoed across the disc.

"Droplet! Droplet! Are you safe?"

"I'm safe. I did it, Moss. We did it. Everyone's okay," Droplet said.

She dabbed frantically at her eyes. She was still in a public booth, after all.

"Oh thank the stars. You'll have to tell me everything when you're home."

"I will. A proper story," Droplet promised. "And Moss..." She took a deep breath and plunged onward. "I think Harra would be a good part of the team."

Applause burst from the disc. "Oh Droplet, I'm so happy to hear you say that," Moss said. Was she choked up? Was Moss choked up right now? Unthinkable. Droplet wished her own eyes would stop leaking.

"She's a good planner, and she saved me even though she didn't know me."

"If you trust her, that's all the recommendation I need," said Moss. "What about Azera?"

Droplet's heart raced. What about Azera? "I mean...I mean, she's...she's been very helpful, too, and she did save me at least once, and I like her. I would definitely want to keep spending time with her when we get back to the city."

"But?" Moss prompted.

What was the "but"? There had to be one; there had to be a reason why Droplet felt so flustered. "She's a human," Droplet said.

"Is that really the reason?" Moss said. When Droplet didn't respond, Moss said, "You can keep thinking, of course. My advice is to trust your gut."

"And what if my gut is wrong? People could die, Moss," she pleaded—pleaded for what, she didn't know.

"Possibly," Moss said. "But in my experience, when you trust yourself, people tend to live."

Back when she'd still been pretending to have some semblance of a plan, Droplet had been sure that they'd need to flee the city as soon as Harra was retrieved. She had to admit, at least to herself, that taking a few days to recover was vastly preferable.

"My employers have almost certainly fired me by now, so there's no point rushing back," Harra said. She'd found a far-speak bank where she could contact her parents and assure them of her safety.

"They're not going to accept 'kidnapped by cultists' as an excuse?" Droplet asked.

Harra laughed. "If only! No, no, they'll tell me that even if that preposterous story were true, that only proves I was irresponsible for daring to drink in such a dangerous locale, and it was my own fault that I got snatched away." She shrugged. "Rich people. What can you do?"

Now was the perfect moment. Droplet took a deep breath, recalling Moss's faith in her. Best to act and not to think too much. That had gotten her this far. "I could hire you," Droplet blurted out.

Harra's ears flicked. "What for?"

"I pretend to be a rich human. I don't know much about the Ninuthen nobility, and that's always been a bit of a problem with this plan. I have a giant, old manor with nobody to keep it maintained except me and Moss. If you're interested, we could use..." Droplet paused and took a deep breath. "We would be thrilled to have you."

"Droplet!" Azera exclaimed. "You were almost, almost going to ask for help there, weren't you?"

"No," said Droplet.

"Mmmmmhm."

Harra rolled her eyes at Azera. "I'd love to clean up your giant, crumbling manor. Can I lecture you on etiquette?"

"Yes. Frequently," Droplet said.

"Will you listen to the lectures?" Azera asked.

"I'll have you know that I can be the model of propriety when the mission calls for it," Droplet said.

"I'll believe it when I see it," Azera said.

That could have been an opening. But Droplet let it pass.

After a few days, the three of them bid goodbye to Mother Enneth and Rangitam. Rangitam snuffled all over Droplet's shoulder, and Droplet promised that she'd join the calls with Moss to say hi. Mother Enneth thanked them for "the most eventful midsummer I've had in at least eleven years" and promised they would be welcome anytime.

They took a boat home. The captain didn't ask many questions. Droplet actually began to relax once they were at sea, enjoying the wind and sun on her face as they sailed under a clear summer sky.

"What are you going to do when you get back to the city?" Droplet asked Azera. They sat at the stern of the boat with Harra, tossing stale bread to the gulls that wheeled in the boat's wake. They were never far out of sight of land, but at this moment, nothing broke the line of blue horizon.

"I've had a carpentry shop of my own for a while. My fiancée couldn't get me to close it down, and I have some commissions from family friends still in the works. People will be curious enough or nosy enough to visit me with odd jobs even while my parents and I are quarreling. The old folks in the neighborhood will bring me some food and try to get me to talk that way. My parents will be less mad eventually. I'll get by."

"That's...good," Droplet said.

Harra's eyes and ears were trained on Droplet. She pretended not to notice. After some silence, Harra sniffed, twitching her whiskers, and pointed to some dolphin fins in the distance.

That night, with a bowl of stars overhead, the three of them lay on the deck to spot constellations. Azera and Harra weren't very good at it, so they began inventing new ones. "Over there, the iconic Child Messing Up Yesterday's Laundry, surely you know that one? And above us, just below the North Star, it's the Three-Quarters Sprackle-Head Screwdriver, a legend among us simple human folk."

Droplet harrumphed and announced she'd tell a real star-story and regaled them with one of the old star-walker tales that had been passed down for thousands of years among shapeshifters—how Aiep and Mianyi fought to control a world where the oceans burned and the skies rained fire.

The three passengers lay quietly after that, simply gazing up.

"Azera," Droplet said, "where are you going to live when we get back?"

"The workshop has a loft I've used before. It's cozy."

"Good, good," said Droplet. She thought she heard Harra sigh, but when she looked over, both Harra and Azera were still looking at the stars.

Two days later, they arrived at the docks of Ninuthen toward evening. The water and the shore echoed with the chaos of hundreds of people trying to execute unrelated plans. Droplet insisted on walking with Azera and Harra back to their neighborhood. Harra would spend a week with her family before heading to Droplet's manor.

Droplet had planned to drop the two off at Harra's place and leave, but at least a dozen different half-cats all *needed* to hug her and cry and exclaim how grateful they were. Before she knew it, she'd agreed to stay for dinner, a boisterous affair that involved five different families dropping in as the celebration for Harra's return drew more and more friends. Early on, Azera, Droplet, and Harra were separated in the crowd, but plenty of friendly strangers asked about their adventure and plied Droplet with food. Harra's father briefly left his daughter's side to insist that Droplet eat. A couple of very serious children asked Droplet to referee their game of hopscotch. It was almost like being back home with her colony.

The food, drink, and talk flowed well into the night. When people began to filter away to their homes, Droplet started making her goodbyes.

"I'll see you soon," she said to Harra.

"See you. And thank you," Harra said. "I still don't think 'thank you' is sufficient, but I haven't yet figured out a suitable addition."

"You'll find a way to return the favor, I'm sure," Droplet said. "And...have you seen Azera?"

Harra steered her through the ramshackle house, around the remaining knots of people, until they found Azera deep in conversation. Harra shouted, "Azera! Get over here!" and vanished back into the house before Droplet could protest.

Azera left her own conversation, coming up to Droplet with a smile.

"I...uh...I'm headed out for the night," Droplet said. "I wanted to say goodbye."

"Oh," Azera said. "I guess it's that time, huh? I'll walk you to the door."

They moved in silence through the jubilant home. *What is there to say?* Droplet thought. *We will see each other again, I'm sure. We had an adventure together, but it's over now.*

At the same time, another part of Droplet's brain thought, *You fool.*

They reached the door, exiting into the balmy summer night. "Well...goodbye, then," Azera said. After one more long look, she turned toward the door.

For a moment, Droplet saw a whole future unfurl before her: Azera would walk through the door and out of Droplet's life, and missions would be easier without the risk of losing someone she cared about, and she'd go back home to an empty manor without even ghosts to keep her company.

Droplet took a deep breath.

"Azera," Droplet said.

Azera spun back around. "Yes?"

"I'd be as good as dead if not for you. Probably dead, honestly. I don't know how I possibly could have done this without you, and I wouldn't want to do it alone anyway. I don't know who I'm going after next, but I want you there with me. If you want. I...I'd like your help. Please?"

There was that smile again. The clocks had struck midnight, but the sun had risen.

"I thought you'd never ask," said Azera. "Yes."

Acknowledgements

I've been working toward a published novel for so long that at the moment I am writing these acknowledgments, I'm feeling grateful to everyone and everything. I will try to summarize.

Many thanks go to Nina Waters, for bringing Duck Prints Press into existence and getting this book out into the world; Hermit for a delightful layout and reminding me that yes, I do get to have opinions on fonts; and Roiu for the incredible cover. Thank you to all my internet writing homes over the years, from the NTWF to the server that I continue to think of as "the Oh No server." I would not be here without the romance channel in the Slack, which sparked the idea that would become *Many Drops Make a Stream*; offline, I am forever grateful to Jessica for forming our real-world writers' group and to Nadeesha for all the pandemic twalks. They and the many friends who beta read for me over the years have helped polish up the rough drafts of this story into the final book.

Thank you to my family—my sisters, for always asking to see my writing, especially in all those years when I refused to show you. Thank you to my parents, who have always had faith in me and also instilled a love of books and animals.

And finally, thank you to my husband, Carter, who makes sure I eat, tells me to rest, assures me that everything will be okay, and helps make my dreams a reality.

Backers

OUR TOP-TIER PATREON BACKERS:

Anonymous Backer
Sam Brown
Tina Houck
jumblejen
Aria L.
Karen Welborn

About The Author:
Adrian Harley

Adrian Harley is an almost-lifelong North Carolinian and a fantasy-fiction aficionado who started delving deep into fandom as an adult. They are an editor of research by day and a writer, also by day. They go to bed early. They have short stories in OFIC Magazine and multiple Duck Prints Press anthologies. They live with their husband and a perfectly reasonable number of cats.

LINKS

Website: https://adrianharley.com
TikTok: https://www.tiktok.com/@aharleywriter
Tumblr: https://adrianharley.tumblr.com

ANTHOLOGIES INCLUDING ADRIAN HARLEY

And Seek (Not) to Alter Me: Queer Fanworks Inspired by Shakespeare's Much Ado About Nothing (author contributor)

She Wears the Midnight Crown (author and editor)

About Duck Prints Press LLC

Duck Prints Press LLC is an independent publisher based in New York State. Our founding vision is to help fanwork creators navigate the complex process of bringing their original works from first draft to print, culminating in publishing their work under our imprint. We are particularly dedicated to working with queer creators and publishing stories and artwork featuring characters from across the LGBTQIA+ spectrum.

Support Duck Prints Press on Patreon and get a bonus epilogue about Droplet and Azera! You'll also get monthly short stories by Press contributors, input on future anthology topics, behind-the-scenes updates on what the Press is working on, coupons for purchases on the Press's site, access to the Press Discord, and more!

Find us online at our website https://duckprintspress.com/ or on social media:

Bluesky: duckprintspress.bsky.social
Facebook: duckprintspress
Instagram: duckprintspress
TikTok: @duckprintspress
Tumblr: @duckprintspress

Goodreads:
https://www.goodreads.com/user/show/129902473-duck-prints-press-llc
Storygraph: https://app.thestorygraph.com/profile/unforth

If you enjoyed this story, don't forget to leave us a review!

www.ingramcontent.com/pod-product-compliance
Lightning Source LLC
Chambersburg PA
CBHW050344030726
47503CB00008B/2606